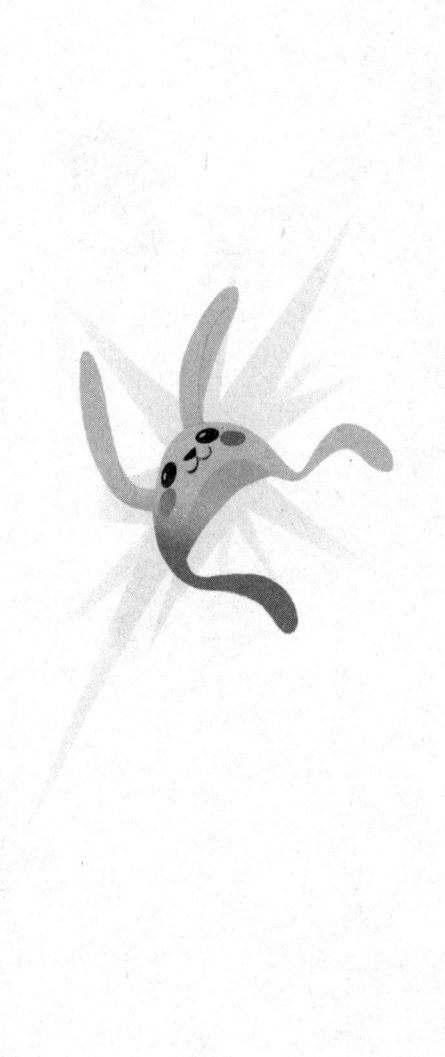

SKYLAR
AND THE K-POP PRINCIPAL

LUAN GOLDIE

WALKER BOOKS

This is a work of fiction. Names, characters, places, and incidents are either products of the author's imagination or, if real, are used fictitiously.

Text copyright © 2024 by Luan Goldie
Illustrations copyright © 2024 by Amy Nguyen

All rights reserved. No part of this book may be reproduced, transmitted, or stored in an information retrieval system in any form or by any means, graphic, electronic, or mechanical, including photocopying, taping, and recording, without prior written permission from the publisher.

First US edition 2025

Library of Congress Control Number: 2024944054
ISBN 978-1-5362-4112-9

24 25 26 27 28 29 SHD 10 9 8 7 6 5 4 3 2 1

Printed in Chelsea, MI, USA

This book was typeset in ITC Berkeley Oldstyle.

Walker Books US
a division of
Candlewick Press
99 Dover Street
Somerville, Massachusetts 02144

www.walkerbooksus.com

EU Authorized Representative: HackettFlynn Ltd., 36 Cloch Choirneal, Balrothery, Co. Dublin, K32 C942, Ireland. EU@walkerpublishinggroup.com

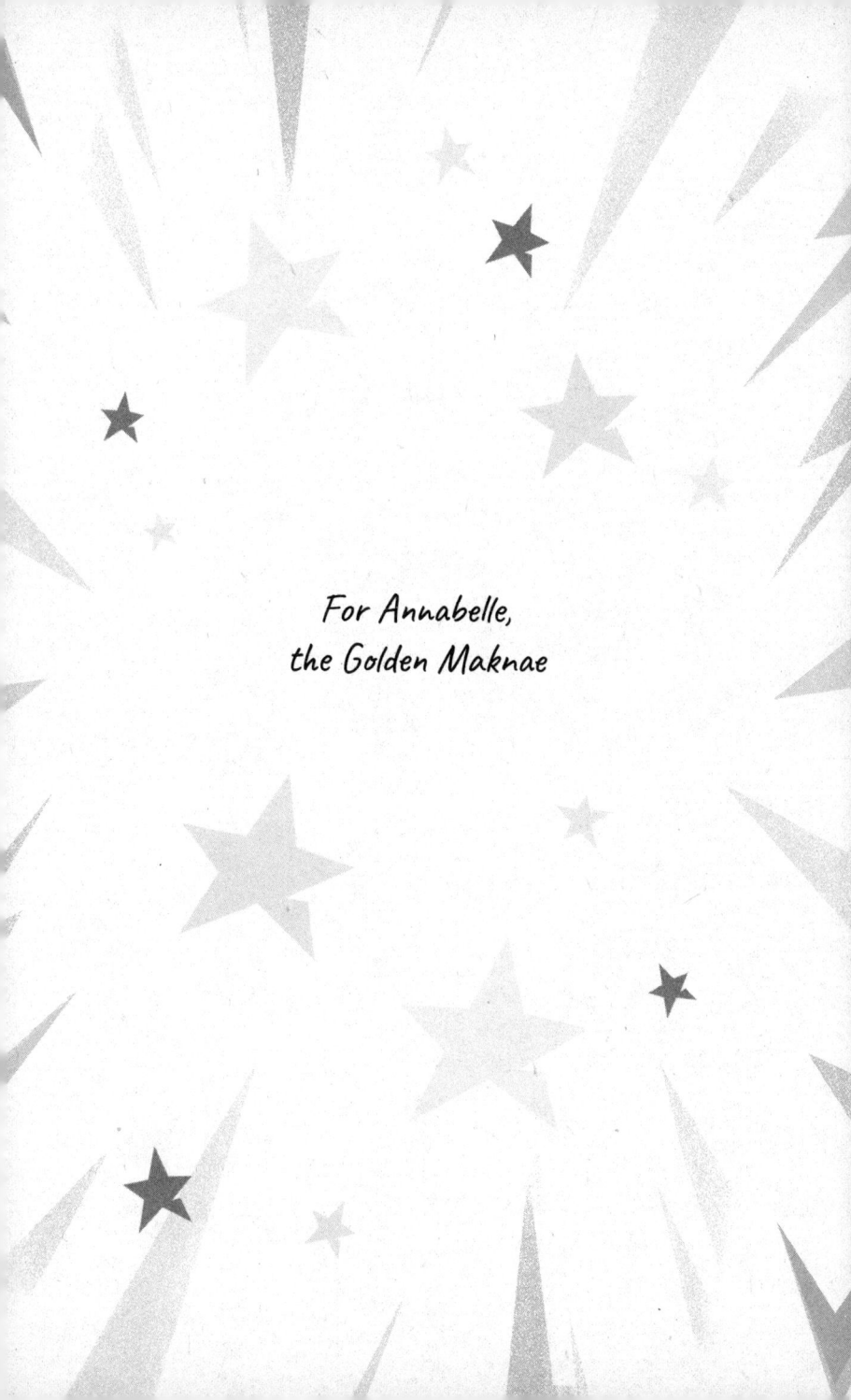

For Annabelle,
the Golden Maknae

1
APPROPRIATELY OBSESSED

My eyes ping open as Kookie scratches at my bedroom door and lets out her weird meow, which sounds nothing like a meow but more like an airplane tumbling from the sky.

"*Neeowww.*"

"Ugh," I moan as I roll over to grab my phone off the charger. It takes a few minutes to turn on as it's old. So old. It belonged to Dad, then Mom, then my brother, Jesse. It even belonged to Nana at one point, but she was too embarrassed to be seen in public with it, so it was agreed that before it was sent to the Museum of Historical Objects, I could have it.

When it finally comes to life, I'm greeted by Woojin's megawatt smile.

"Good morning," I mumble as I kiss the screen. Now, of course I love all eight members of AZ8, the best boy band on the planet, equally. But Woojin is my favorite because he has the best hair and loves small animals.

I have four new messages, all from Dana, my best friend and fellow fangirl. First message:

> **Dana:** Morning!!! Happy Monday. Are you awake? Are you excited? I'm SO excited!

AZ8 is making a video comeback this evening, and while this is very exciting, Dana is generally an excited kind of person. Second message:

> **Dana:** I LITERALLY can't eat breakfast.

Third message:

> **Dana:** So EXCITED I just buttered a tea bag.

Fourth message:

> **Dana:** Michyeosseo!

Michyeosseo? While I listen to around a hundred hours a week of K-pop, also known as Korean pop music, I still rely on online translators for even the most basic of words. Hmm, let's see: *michyeosseo* means *crazy*. I text back:

> **Me:** Annyeonghaseyo!

Which means *hello* and is the longest Korean word I know how to spell. I really struggle with languages and have recently concluded that, like soccer and breaststroke, languages are something I'm incapable of learning. Along with piano, singing in tune, ice-skating, boiling eggs, and 99.9 percent of mathematical concepts. Hmm, it's actually a really long list . . .

Kookie scratches at the bedroom door. "*Neeee-owwww.*"

"Skylar," Dad shouts, "*your* cat is crying."

I stick out my arm from under the duvet and pull open the door handle, which I can easily reach from my bed because I have the tiniest box room ever made. That's not a complaint, because my room is perfect. I have a big bed covered with the plushies I've dedicated the last two years of my life to collecting, a shelf where I safely store my 160-page ring binder of AZ8 photocards, a window that overlooks a bakery—can you imagine the smells?!—and every inch of wall space is covered with beautiful photos and posters of AZ8.

Kookie bounds in, climbs on my chest, and pads right up to my face.

"Morning, Kookie."

"I'm not happy!" Dad shouts from the doorway. He's got his bright red running shoes on, which means either he's going for a run, or he'll spend the whole day *talking* about going for a run. "That beast," he says, pointing at Kookie, who is now covering my face with fishy licks, "has done her business in my yucca plant."

Yikes.

Dad loves his plants. Sometimes, when I watch him stroke the leaves one by one with a damp cloth and tell them about his day, I think he loves them more than he loves Mom.

"My poor yucca. It's never going to grow if that feline keeps using it as her toilet."

"I'm sorry, Dad. I forgot to let her out last night. I fell asleep watching *Go Go AZ8!* It was a really funny episode. Tae and Jungwon had a challenge to make spicy Korean seafood soup while being sprayed with water guns and—"

"It's your animal, Skylar," Dad grumbles, cutting me off before I can tell him how hysterical it was seeing

Jungwon add sugar instead of salt to the soup. "And shouldn't you be at school by now?"

I shake my head. "It's seven o'clock, so no."

Dad rubs his belly and looks confused. "Seven? No wonder I'm so hungry. I'd better be getting lunch ready."

Lunch at seven in the morning? Yeah, that's not unusual in this house. I live with a bunch of adults who have no concept of time. Dad drives night buses, so for him anything that happens after six a.m. is classified as late. Then there's my older brother, Jesse. He stays out most nights and returns home at odd times of the day saying things like "Is it Wednesday?" Nana is also questionable, because in the five years since she came to live with us, I've never seen her go to bed. She just stays up all night reading cookbooks and watching reality shows where rich women shout at each other. Finally, there's Mom. I have no clue what time she wakes up. Though I once got up at half past five in the morning and she was already fully dressed and on her second cup of coffee.

I put on my disgusting school uniform—a tan pleated skirt, a boxy brown blazer, a mucus-colored shirt, and, the most unforgivable part, mustard socks—and head into the living room, also known as Mom's textile HQ. After losing her job with the city last year,

Mom became a mompreneur and set up her own company, Cushy Cushions, which is great except for when she has a big order and I have to help out.

She's sitting at her sewing machine with her headphones on, and, judging by the way she's got a hand on her forehead, she's listening to one of her romantic audiobooks.

"Valentino's a scoundrel," she mutters. "Don't trust him."

Mom jumps as I tap her on the shoulder.

"Skylar." She stops to pull off her headphones. "You're still here?"

I resist the urge to sigh. "Yep."

"Darling, it's so late. Shouldn't you be at Bright and Brainy Breakfast Club?"

I shake my head, because it's now only seven fifteen and Bright and Brainy Breakfast Club stopped having me in for Nutella on toast when they realized I wasn't bright *or* brainy.

"If I'd known you were still here, you could have helped me. Your tiny hands are perfect for stitching on sequins." She tuts and looks at her teetering pile of sewing. "Never mind, you can help after school."

I shake my head quickly. "I can't. I'm going to Dana's after school."

"Anyone seen Jesse recently?" Dad asks as he comes in.

"Not since Saturday night," Mom says. "He was going to a festival, I think."

Dad looks out the window at the heavy rain. "Hardly the weather for it."

"Mom, AZ8 is launching their video comeback in less than twelve hours. Dana and I have the whole evening planned."

She shrugs. "You can watch your three-minute music video while helping me sew."

What is she talking about? It's so much more than a three-minute video. For us AZ8 fans, known as Glows, a video comeback is a whole experience—an experience that consists of:

1. Learning the dance routine. AZ8's brilliant dance routines take hours of dedicated practice to learn, but I usually pick up most moves on the first day. I've been dancing since before I could walk. I literally stood up at six months old, went "Goo-goo-gah!" and did the running man.

2. Working with Glows all over the world to break records. The last AZ8 video had one hundred million views in one day. Mom said the majority of those were probably me and Dana.

3. Learning the words. AZ8 songs are mostly in Korean but you can just mumble "hmm-hmm-hmm" until the English chorus kicks in.

4. Arguing about which member looks the best and who your bias is: this means your favorite. Mine is obviously Woojin.

5. Talking online with other Glows about all of the above.

You do all this repeatedly until a non-Glow, usually a parent, shouts something like "My ears are bleeding. Make it stop!"

I live for video comebacks. How can Mom suggest I miss one to help her sew cushion covers? It's bad enough that despite being AZ8's number one fan I'm not going to their concert this Saturday. The reality of this hurts, but Dad said one ticket costs as much as our electricity bill, plus our city tax (whatever that is), plus a year's worth of vet bills. Also, the tickets sold out in four minutes and six seconds.

I sigh, making sure it's long enough and dramatic enough to get both of my parents' attention.

"It's just a band, Skylar," Dad says while spritzing his bonsai. A bonsai, in case you don't know, is a tiny Barbie-size tree. "Don't you ever get bored of watching those boys sing, dance, and eat noodles?"

What a ridiculous question. "Don't you ever get bored of watching that tiny tree not grow?" I snap back.

Mom laughs. "When I was your age, liking a pop star never took up this much time. We watched their videos once a week on TV if we were lucky. There wasn't all this extra stuff to do."

"I can help you sew another day," I offer. "Just any day that's not this week."

"And according to this, you have a math test on Friday," Dad says, tapping the Saint Margaret's academic wall calendar.

Hmm, he's right, I *do* have a math test, but it's not an important one or anything. Plus, I'm already in the bottom ranking for math—what's another bad mark going to do? Send me back to elementary school?

Mom unrolls some sparkly fabric. "You can come straight home today. Help me, do some math, and then spend a bit of quality time with Nana."

Nana loves "quality time," which basically involves me chopping onions, unwrapping a ton of seasoning cubes, and listening to her tell stories about her childhood.

"You'll need to be home to repot my yucca plant too," Dad adds while doing some very deep lunges.

"Sorry," I say. "I really can't do cushions or cooking or math or replanting yuccas this evening. Tonight is all about AZ8."

"Enough," Mom snaps, now getting angry. "You're wasting too much time on those boys."

"Mom, AZ8's literally the only thing I care about."

She shakes her head. "That's the problem, Skylar. You're too obsessed."

"Yes, but *appropriately* obsessed," I clarify.

"It's time to take a break."

Dad nods. "I agree. Also, I'm not ready to hear another K-pop song on repeat for months."

"What are you saying?" I shout. And quickly realize my mistake, because raised voices are not tolerated in *this* house.

Mom looks at Dad and they do this weird thing where it's like they're speaking to each other without saying any words. Eventually they both nod, turn to me, and say at the same time, "AZ8 is banned."

2
BRAVERY GETS YOU NOWHERE

Dad was right about the weather, and by the time I walk through the grand entrance of Saint Margaret's Academy my shoes are soaked right through to my ugly mustard socks. Though soggy feet are nothing compared to the deep sinking feeling I have inside.

One whole week without AZ8.

Seven *horrible* days.

No posters. No plushies. No gazing at photocards. No phone and no watching video comebacks.

The only thing I managed to grab before my parents ransacked my room and my life was my light-up dancing bunny ears hat, which I stuffed in my backpack. Ugh. How am I going to tell Dana that I can't watch the video comeback?

I sit through an especially confusing assembly titled "Cybercrime: Don't Do It!" while shivering in my wet shoes as the forefathers of Saint Margaret's stare down at me from the massive oil paintings that hang around the hall.

Saint Margaret's was founded by Sir Charles Callus after he returned from the war—I'm not sure which war, but I suspect he wasn't on the right side. He's the one who came up with the school motto: "Achieve or hang your head in shame." There have been five other Callus principals since then, though I imagine our current one, Ms. Callus, is the meanest and pushiest of them all. Her portrait is the biggest, and even though some say she's smiling in it, I've always felt she's 49 percent smirking, 51 percent snarling.

At lunchtime I'm trying to digest Monday's Mexican Mania menu when Dana finally comes out of her honors classes.

"We have got to do something about this," she grumbles as she slides into the chair across from mine.

I nod. "I know. I hate that we have hardly any classes together. Why can't you be less smart?"

"No, I'm talking about climate change," Dana says as she holds out long wet strands of her bright red hair. "It's making the water cycle do weird things. Flash floods, droughts, extreme thunderstorms. And look at this." She thrusts a plastic spork in my face. "Do you know how long plastic cutlery takes to decompose? And on what planet do you need a spork to eat a chili bean wrap?" She pauses for a breath. "I've sent you twenty-seven messages. Why haven't you replied?"

"Dana," I start, but can't find the right words to break it to her. Since the first day of sixth grade, when we both flicked finger hearts at each other across the assembly hall, we've shared every AZ8 moment.

"It's my parents," I say.

Dana gasps. "Oh no, are they splitting up? Did your dad lose his job? Is the bonsai dead?"

I shake my head. "No. Worse. They've grounded me."

"But I've already made a secure booking with my family to have the living room for the video comeback." She grimaces. "Does this mean we have to watch it at your house?"

We both know this isn't something that works. It's really hard to enjoy AZ8 at my house with Dad sitting there saying things like "I can dance better than that" and "Ooh, are baggy pants back in fashion?"

I take a deep breath. "I can't watch the video comeback at all. My parents have banned AZ8 from my life."

Dana's eyes go wide. "No! Why?"

I shrug. "They think I'm obsessed."

"You *are* obsessed. That's the whole point of being a Glow."

"They think I spend too much time on AZ8 when I should be studying fractions and removing poop from greenery and using my tiny hands to sew."

"You do have remarkably tiny hands," she agrees.

"Dana, this is serious."

"How long is this ban for?"

"An entire whole week."

"A *week*? That's one hundred and sixty-eight hours without K-pop." Dana slams the table. "Are they insane? Isn't it bad enough that we can't go to the concert on Saturday?"

I take my light-up dancing bunny ears hat from my backpack and pull it on. "This is all I have left." It's the same hat Woojin wore in episode one hundred and twenty-four of *Go Go AZ8!* Except mine isn't from some supercool shop in South Korea, but from a website called Discounted Fake Stuff that Nana loves to shop at. Sometimes when I squeeze the pumps to make the ears dance it short-circuits and gives me a tiny electric shock.

Dana chuckles as I make the ears move.

The bell signaling the end of lunch rings, and

we clear away our nonrecyclables and make our way through the damp halls to our next class. Dana talks the whole way about how to solve the double catastrophes of climate change and being grounded until a seventh-grade girl with freckles and a large unibrow hisses, "Shh, Ms. Callus is here."

"Hurry along now, students," Ms. Callus shrieks in her super-high-pitched voice.

Our principal stands at the foot of the stairs, rosy-cheeked and wearing a pink twinset complete with pearl necklace and a huge helmet of gray hair. Sure, she might look like a sweet old grandma, but it's all a front. Ms. Callus is a true wolf in sheep's clothing, a bully in a blouse, a menace in magenta, a threat in floral.

"Young man," she screeches at a slouchy boy in front of us. "This is not a day at the beach. Chin up. Look lively."

The boy hoists his shoulders up hurriedly in an attempt to stand soldier-straight.

Ms. Callus loves good posture; she also loves perfection, achievement, and triumph. Sounds good, doesn't it? Until you find out what she doesn't love. So far, I have found this list to include individuality, creativity, happiness, averageness, and children. She especially dislikes average children, as she reminded everyone last week when she sent a letter home headed *How to be the best in a world filled with losers*.

"Time is ticking," she trills, "and tardiness robs one of opportunities."

As we get closer, she turns her beady eyes on us and her face hardens.

"Stop," she commands icily. She raises a finger and points a pink fingernail right at me. "What. Is. That?"

"Er . . . my head?" I reply.

Ms. Callus gasps. "Do you think you are a comedian, young lady? Does the world look like your stage?"

I glance at Dana, whose eyes go wide as she mouths something at me. I try to read her lips. I think she's saying *your mat*. Or *you're a cat*. Maybe *ugly bats*? I'm not sure, but while I'm trying to work it out Ms. Callus shouts, "Surrender that violation of uniform policy immediately!"

Oh. My dancing bunny ears hat. My hands feel jittery as I pull it off and clumsily try to stuff it into my bag. "Sorry, Ms. Callus, I forgot I had it on."

From all around me there's giggling, and I feel my face burn hot with embarrassment.

Ms. Callus snatches the hat from the opening of my bag. "What a monstrosity!" She holds it up by one of the ears as if it were diseased. "If I ever catch you flagrantly flouting the rules of this fine establishment again, you will find yourself expelled. Do I make myself clear?"

"Yes," I squeak.

"Yes who?"

"Yes, Ms. Callus."

"Very well," she says. "Now move along."

Dana takes me by the arm as we walk on. I'm shaking—I hate being shouted at and having everyone stare at me.

"I'm sorry that happened," Dana says sympathetically, and gives my arm a squeeze.

"Me too," I mutter miserably. "This is turning out to be a truly terrible day."

"At least we have a class together now. Computing, yeah!"

I raise an eyebrow at her. "You hate computing."

"Only because it's the single hour of the schedule where I feel I'm losing neurons rather than generating them."

As we enter the computer lab, Mr. Keen is sitting on his desk and combing his facial hair. "Hey, dudes," he calls as we take our seats. "Make sure you all sign the register-rooney and then we'll get stuck into some awesome algorithms."

"Register-*rooney*?" Dana repeats with a groan. "Oh, this is already horrible."

"Who's ready for some fun with the fundamental principles of computer science?" he shouts enthusiastically.

Dana rolls her eyes and whispers, "I can't believe I need to be here. How did Mr. Keen ever qualify as a computing teacher? Last week he called a microchip a microwave."

Mr. Keen bounces toward us. "Skylar, you haven't turned on the thingamajig yet."

"You mean . . . the computer?" Dana says.

Mr. Keen laughs. "Your brain amazes me, Dana Popa."

I turn on my computer, though nothing can turn my heart back on after what just happened.

Mr. Keen looks at me and tips his head to one side. "What's up, kiddo? Usually you dance right in here. Why so glum? I hope you know you can always talk to me, because I'm not just your teacher"—he sprays his beard with a minty-smelling mist—"I'm also your friend."

"Ms. Callus shouted at Skylar for wearing a K-pop dancing bunny ears hat on school property," Dana explains.

"A what?"

Dana gets out her phone—because you're totally allowed to use your phone in Mr. Keen's class—and shows him a photo of Woojin in the hat.

"Whoa, that's a supercool accessory," Mr. Keen says.

"Very retro, funky, manga, swish swish." He rummages in his pocket and takes out a packet of bubble gum. "Hubba Bubba?"

"No thanks," I say. "I'm too depressed to enjoy Atomic Apple right now."

"Sure, sure. We all get that way sometimes. Don't worry about doing any work this lesson. Chill, Alt, Delete."

"That doesn't even make sense," Dana mutters as he wanders off.

A roll of thunder makes everyone jump. The rain is epic, falling so fast it looks like one big sheet of heavy grayness. I feel down, so very down. First my AZ8 plushies, posters, and photocards; then my phone; and now my dancing bunny ears hat. This really is the worst day ever.

"What does Ms. Callus do with all those confiscated items anyway?" I ask.

Dana huffs. "I heard she has a ritual burning in the science garden every Friday. A huge bonfire of lipsticks, iPhones, and Uno cards. Can you imagine how toxic those fumes are?"

I picture Ms. Callus in the science garden, her head flung back as she laughs hysterically while my beautiful 100 percent polyester hat bursts into flames.

"I'm so fed up with adults," I seethe.

"Me too, Skylar. My parents are point-blank refusing to invest in an electric car. What don't they understand about being carbon-neutral?"

I slam my hand down on the desk. "They don't care."

"Well, they should. Because *I* wasn't the one taking all those cheap flights to Ibiza. Or cooking pasta with the pot lid off. Or taking bubble baths. Or—"

The thunder claps again.

"See?" Dana gestures outside. "Mother Nature is going bananas and what are we doing? Eating wraps with plastic sporks."

"You're right; you are *so* right." I pause. "What *are* we doing?"

Dana squints at the learning objective Mr. Keen has scrawled on the board. "We're learning how to edit an online grocery shop."

"No, really, what are we doing? These ridiculous adults are always telling *us* what to do and how *we* should be living our lives. When to wake up, when to study, when to eat, when it's time to switch off *Go Go AZ8!* even though it's the best episode ever and you've only seen it four times that day."

Dana puts a hand on my shoulder. "Breathe, Skylar."

I can't. I'm so angry right now. "We need to start

standing up for ourselves." And with this, I stand up.

Dana looks worried. "Are you going to do something impulsive?"

"I'm going to confront Ms. Callus. I'm going to tell her it's not OK to shout at me in front of the whole school just for wearing a hat to express myself and keep my head warm."

"She's the principal. Shouting is probably article 2.4 in her job description."

"It's not right," I say. "This school supposedly teaches respect. That wasn't respect. Are you with me?"

"Skylar, I can't get into trouble. I'm . . ." Dana drops her head and touches the gold badge on her blazer. "I'm on student council."

"Fine," I snap. "I'll go on my own. Mr. Keen, can I go to the restroom, please?"

Mr. Keen pops his Atomic Apple gum and makes a double gun with his fingers. "Sure thing, kiddo. Take as long as you need."

"Skylar"—Dana grabs my hand—"don't do it."

"I have to make a stand. Plus, I want my hat back."

The only sound in the hallway is that of the rain pounding against the windows. It's almost creepy. I walk past class after class filled with kids chanting Spanish verbs, reciting ancient poems, and solving quadratic equations. I pause by a huge banner that reads HARD WORK CONQUERS ALL. Under it are hundreds of photos of all the top students, each one the best or quickest or first at doing something.

I'll never make it onto this display.

"You!" a familiar voice yelps.

The whole reason I'm out of class is to find Ms. Callus, but now that I have, my heart jumps out of my chest.

Her pastel-colored kitten heels slowly click down the hall toward me. Though not slowly enough for me to work out a plan of what to say. She stops in front of me and I notice my hat is slung over the top of the pink leather handbag that dangles from her arm.

"Why are you out of class?" she demands.

The thunder rumbles, rattling the window frames and making me wonder just how *michyeosseo* I am. I take a deep breath. "I came to get my hat back," I announce bravely.

Ms. Callus's mouth turns down and she looks at me like I'm an extra helping of overcooked broccoli. "You're in sixth grade, aren't you?" she sneers. "I detest sixth graders. Always complaining that middle school is not as fun as elementary school. That there's too much moving around and not enough glitter and making things from old egg cartons."

"That's not true," I protest weakly.

"What's wrong, little sixth grader? Is it that teachers don't act like your mommy?" she says in a whiny voice that I think is meant to sound like me. Rude. Ms. Callus is the one with the whiny voice here.

"My hat?" I nod toward it. "I want it back. Please."

A flash of lightning illuminates Ms. Callus's face, and she looks as if she's about to dish out a lifetime of detention. "What's your name?" she demands with a sneer.

I swallow hard. "Skylar Smith."

She turns her pointy nose up. "A little nobody. You're not one of the high achievers, the top students, the award winners, the worker bees who are helping to cement my legacy as one of the greatest educators of all time."

She steps closer and I can smell her flowery perfume, like a park during peak hay-fever season. I don't know what comes over me. Maybe it's the rage that has been building all morning, the crazy weather, or the chili bean wrap, but I lurch forward and grab my hat.

"How dare you?" Ms. Callus screeches.

"It belongs to me," I say firmly as I put it on my head where it belongs.

"It is a banned item. Now, TAKE IT OFF!"

"No," I retort, and I make the bunny ears dance.

With each flip of the ears Ms. Callus gets angrier and angrier. "Silly little girl, that's enough!" she screams.

"No! I'm fed up with adults telling me how to live my life. I wish I was in charge."

"You wouldn't last a second!" she yells.

"Yes, I would. Your life is easy. I wish I had it. Do you hear me? I said I wish I had your life! I wish I was in charge!"

I feel the familiar sensation of the hat short-circuiting, and a little shock tickles my hairline. I furiously press again and again to make the ears flip, and Ms. Callus finally explodes. She grabs the hat by the ears as a tingle runs down my face and body.

Suddenly a huge flash of green light shoots down the middle of the hall, zigging and zagging like Sonic having an identity crisis. The light turns bright white, then surrounds us and lifts us off the ground.

"What's happening?" I shout, panic filling me as Ms. Callus and I swirl around in some kind of luminous vortex.

"I don't know!" she shouts back, her eyes wide. "But

whoever is responsible is getting their parents called in."

BOOM!

The white light bursts into thousands of tiny stars.

I try to scream, but my voice is lost to a strange fizzing noise, until . . .

SNAP!

Everything goes dark.

3
THAT WOMAN HAS MY FACE

I open my eyes. I'm still in the hallway. Though I'm now on the floor, propped against the wall. And opposite me is . . . Well, it's me. Also slumped on the floor, leaning against the wall.

Am I looking in a mirror? I move my right hand slowly but the *me* opposite doesn't. No. Not a mirror.

I've bumped my head. Hard.

Yes, that's it; I've bumped my head very hard and now I've gone crazy.

"I'm having an out-of-body experience," I murmur. My voice sounds different. It sounds like, well, a high-pitched sort of annoying whiny sound. It sounds like . . .

It sounds like Ms. Callus.

Ms. Callus? She was with me when that huge flash of light happened. Where is she now?

I try to stand but it takes me ages to push myself up, and my knees make a weird clicking noise as I do.

I look again at myself. Yes. Myself. Now standing opposite me. I'm confused. So very, very confused.

"I think I need a doctor," I say faintly. Again, the voice is not mine.

What is happening? The version of *me*, the one standing opposite, the one I am clearly imagining—*hallucinating*—is touching *her* face, grabbing *her* cheeks, and clawing at *her* hair.

I hold my arms out and see pink sleeves with wrinkly hands sticking out of the cuffs, a gold watch reading 2:22, nails polished pink, and, clutched in the hands, my dancing bunny ears hat. I look down at the horrendously flowered flowing skirt and pastel tights and, the worst part, sensible pumps with a kitten heel. When I look back up, back up at myself who is not really *me* but someone else entirely, I scream.

We both do.

Both of me.

Are you following what's happening?

Because I don't think I am.

In fact, I'm really very baffled right now.

I scream like I'm watching the scariest horror movie ever, like I'm convinced I'm not buckled in properly on a ten-looping roller coaster, like when I had a dream AZ8 was breaking up, like when we first got Kookie and she did a tiny poop on my pillow.

"Soul mates before student council!"

At the sound of Dana's voice, I turn to see my best friend running down the hall.

"I'm coming, Skylar. Don't you worry; I'm com—OH!" Dana's eyes widen as she spots me. She folds at the waist and mumbles, "I'm so sorry, Ms. Callus. Please forgive me for being out of class and for raising my voice above acceptable indoor level and—"

"What are you doing?" I interrupt. "Why are you bending over like that?"

"I'm bowing, Ms. Callus, and asking you to please not judge my momentary lapse in behavior."

"Will you stop acting so *michyeosseo* right now!"

Dana flicks back up like a jack-in-the-box and gawks at me. "Huh?"

I hold my arms out again, this time noticing little brown spots on my hands. Old-lady hands. "I'm not Ms. Callus!" I cry. "Actually, I think I am. But really, I'm not."

Dana's gaze ricochets between me and the fake me

opposite. "Uh, Skylar?" she says, trying to stare into my soul. "Is that you?"

I nod. "I think so."

"Then who is . . ."

We both turn to look at what's going on opposite. The fake me is patting her hair and standing with her mouth agape in a very unflattering way, and mumbling "This is impossible!" over and over again.

Dringggg! The bell. The signal that in seconds the hallway will be filled with students.

"Oh my Greta Thunberg!" Dana exclaims. "We need to get you two out of here."

With lightning speed, Dana drags us both through the fire exit, past the school cafeteria and technology block, and up the back stairs to Ms. Callus's office, which is enormous. It has a huge fancy desk as well as a very serious-looking conference table where, I imagine, the teachers gather and plot ways to keep us all miserable.

I watch myself, who I'm almost certain is now actually Ms. Callus, sink into the big green leather chair behind the desk and groan.

I can't think of anything weirder than seeing my tiny eleven-year-old self sitting in that chair. Until I catch my reflection in the trophy cabinet.

"Oh my gosh," I cry. "Ohmygoshohmygosh." I have

a wrinkly face! I have a stiff helmet of hair! And for some reason, I can't stop scowling.

How did this happen? Why am I suddenly a thousand years old? Why do I look like Ms. Callus?

The other me—who is really Ms. Callus—reaches into the desk drawer and pulls out a small glass and a bottle of brown liquid.

Now, I know some kids want to try alcohol, but Dad gave me a little taste of something called Buck's Fizz once at Christmas and it was terrible, like expired orange juice someone had burped bubbles into.

"Um, yuck, please don't make me drink that," I plead.

Dana stands in the corner of the office and shakes her head. "Body-swapping happens all the time in movies from the olden days, but I never knew it was a real thing." She's excited, and not a normal Dana level of excitement either. *"Eeee!"* she squeals and does a little clap. "The neurotransmitters in my brain are going crazy right now. Dopamine is scrambling all over the place."

I frown at her. "No, Dana, your brain *can't* scramble right now. I need you to explain what's happening here. This is a disaster."

"A disaster," Ms. Callus repeats, using *my* voice, as she tips a second glass of her horrible drink into my healthy young body.

"Wow." Dana steps toward me and pinches my cheeks. "Your skin is all crinkly, like wrapping paper. So wow!"

I slap her hand away. "Stop wowing and start explaining. Why has this happened?"

Dana taps a finger to her lips. "Well, you obviously triggered a body swap between you and Ms. Callus."

"How?" I ask as Ms. Callus groans.

Dana shrugs. "How would I know?"

"Because you know *everything*."

"That's not true, Skylar. It's actually a very common misconception about me."

"Tell me what happens in these old movies. Why do they swap?"

"Because one person thinks the other person doesn't understand them."

I look at Ms. Callus, who's topping off her glass with yet more brown liquid. She definitely doesn't understand me. "OK. Then how do they swap back?"

"They learn," Dana says plainly, as if she's just met me and doesn't yet know I'm someone who finds the concept of learning tricky.

"Learn what? Dana, what do I need to learn?"

"I'm not sure, but I think it's something to do with empathy and walking in the other person's shoes."

"Does it have to be these shoes?" I cry as I look down at the horribly pinchy heels. Panic wells up. "No. Help!"

"Don't shout at me," she grumbles.

"I'm not shouting at you!" I shout.

"Permission to use my cellular device?" Dana asks me.

"Why are you asking me for permission?"

"Because you're the principal."

"I am *not* the principal," I say in my principal voice. "I am me. Skylar. Your bestie. Now get on the internet and find out what's going on."

Ms. Callus lets out a little wail from behind her giant desk. "I'm a sixth grader . . . I'm going to have to go through school again."

"Listen to this," Dana says as she reads from her phone. "'The act of two beings swapping bodies in stories and movies is commonly brought on by extreme incidents or exposure to enchanted objects such as enchanted stones, enchanted fountains, enchanted fortune cookies, enchanted masks, enchanted—'"

"There was no enchantment," I argue. "There was a storm and some yelling over me violating school uniform policy and some lightning . . . yes, green lightning, that's it—that was the extreme incident."

"The lightning," Ms. Callus says. "That's the last thing I remember. I saw a green flash, and when I could see again, I was—"

"Me," I finish. "The lightning made us switch. So, basically, we need to get hit by lightning again."

"Did the lightning actually hit you?" Dana asks doubtfully. "Because lightning strikes kill nine out of ten people and your hair isn't even singed. Also, and I'm not trying to show off with my extensive knowledge of meteorology here, but lightning isn't green. And it can't come inside buildings."

"The child is correct," Ms. Callus says.

"Did either of you utter a magic phrase?" Dana asks.

"No," I answer. "Though I did say something about wanting to be in charge."

Ms. Callus nods. "Yes, that's right. You made some wild claim about how easy my life is compared with yours." She cackles. "Well, forget empathy—you're about to feel exhaustion and stress like never before."

I glare at her. "Yeah, and you're about to feel frustration and powerlessness."

I'm glad she's going to feel some adolescent pain; I'd just rather she didn't have to feel it in *my* body. I sigh as the reality hits me. "When I wished to be in charge, I was thinking more along the lines of being able to stay up late and have unlimited data on my phone. Not this." I indicate my old, decrepit body.

"Calm down," Dana says, "this isn't a forever situation. I'm ninety-eight percent sure these switches are a twenty-four-hour thing, like a stomach bug. Remember when we had that last term, Skylar? I've never been able to look at trail mix the same way again . . ."

I glance at Ms. Callus's watch, which is still stuck at 2:22. "Being an old person for twenty-four hours is far worse than spewing up some snacks," I moan.

"Are you serious?" Dana whispers. "Twenty-four hours as a grown-up could be amazing. Grown-ups have influence. They have money. They have Amazon Prime accounts." She pauses a beat and grins. "And you know what else they have?"

"Bills and frown lines?"

"Freedom." Dana raises a fist in the air. "Freedom to watch AZ8 till their formerly grounded but now sluggishly beating hearts are content."

She's right: me being Ms. Callus means the AZ8 ban doesn't affect me for the next twenty-four hours. Which means I can enjoy their video comeback later. In fact, I could watch it on repeat all night if I wanted. And I do want. Oh yes, I do.

Dana puts her hands on my shoulders and asks the

essential question all Glows must ask themselves when faced with something that scares them. "What would Woojin do?"

"Hit a high note and moonwalk around this very nice oak desk?"

"Exactly. You can do this, Skylar."

I think it over. A whole night and day as someone else.

Dana stares at me and nods. "Am I right, or am I right?"

This all sounds too easy. Surely there are ninety-nine problems we're failing to consider . . . Ah, I have one.

"Ms. Callus, if I go to your house as you, won't your husband notice? Because, honestly, I don't think I'm good wife material, and I'm also not the best liar."

Dana laughs. "It's true. I love this girl like I love Jungwon's hair, but she's the worst liar in the world."

"That's because lying gives me an itchy red rash. It's morally wrong too."

"I don't have time for a husband," Ms. Callus says with a snort. "School is my husband."

"Gross," Dana says.

"Yeah, that is weird," I agree.

"No, it's not. This school is my everything," Ms. Callus says. "This sanctuary of scholarship is the beat of my heart, the blood in my veins, the drive in my—"

"That's why you're mean to us," I say. "You have no work-life balance. Why don't you join a Zumba group or do some community gardening? Do you even have friends?"

"I don't need friends," she snaps. "I have a profession that satisfies me, a cause that sustains, a duty that suffices, a calling that—"

I snap my wrinkly fingers triumphantly. "I knew it. No friends. That explains it all."

"I have many friends," she protests angrily. "I have my secretary, Mr. Idle. He sometimes says hello to me. And the, uh . . . the, uh . . . the milkman, yes. We spoke last Tuesday. My Latin teacher too—she always greets me. You might want to learn some Latin while you're me."

"Latin?" Dana scoffs. "No one has time to learn a dead language right now. We need to start thinking about how to get you both home. To your own homes. Or to each other's homes. Oh, you know what I mean. Ms. Callus, can you drive us?"

"Certainly not. I'm an eleven-year-old girl. I can't be seen behind the wheel of a vintage Jaguar. Plus, I doubt I can reach the pedals."

"Hey," I protest. "I'm almost five foot three. I can't

believe I've got to live in this horrible old body." I touch my hair and my long-held suspicions are proven right: it's helmet hard. What does she put in it anyway? Glue?

Ms. Callus stands. "I think the real issue here is that I am a lady of distinguished tastes and habits. There is simply no way you will be able to convince people *you* are *me*."

I snort. "I'm sure it's not that hard being you. You're the one who's going to struggle being eleven, getting bossed around by adults, stressing about the planet burning up, and going to school *here*!"

"Stop being so dramatic." Ms. Callus pokes at the dancing bunny ears hat on the desk. "Yuck!" she says, then puts it on reluctantly. "See, I'm already so convincing. Now, tell me what I do at your house. My guess is lounge in bed while idly scrolling TikTok."

Dana laughs. "No one uses TikTok anymore."

Ms. Callus clears her throat, which is pointless because there's nothing wrong with *my* throat. "I could be an eleven-year-old with my eyes shut," she boasts. "The problem may come with your parents. Surely they will question why their offspring has suddenly become an incredibly well-spoken and intellectually impressive being."

"My parents are too busy to notice intellectually

impressive beings. As long as you wake up on time for school, feed Kookie the cat, and don't ask Dad if he's managed to go running, you should be fine. Though if you're able to sew sequins into the shape of a champagne glass, that would definitely help."

"Sew? Well, yes, I once read a book on Tudor tapestry and it was really a wonder . . ." She goes on and on and on. Yada, yada, yada.

"Ms. Callus," Dana says politely, "I think it'd be a good idea for us to get off school property now. Is there anything else Skylar needs to know?"

"Yes," Ms. Callus says. "Do keep in mind the many decades I have spent upholding the Callus name while displaying nothing but excellence and nobility. I would appreciate you maintaining my much-revered reputation over the next twenty-four hours."

I put my pinkie finger out, my finger that is now kind of old and creased-looking. "Don't worry, Ms. Callus. I swear on Tae's dimples I'm not going to ruin your name. If anything, I'll make it better. By tomorrow, everyone will think you're cooler than ever."

Ms. Callus sighs. "That's what I'm afraid of," she mutters, before joining her pinkie reluctantly with mine.

4
HOW HOT ARE YOUR FEET?

"I love the Tube," Dana says as she gazes back at the station and smiles. "Two hundred and forty-nine miles of tracks and over half a million mice. Epic."

"I hate the Tube," I grumble. "All those adults pushing and shoving and tutting and coughing and pressing their armpits into one another's faces while eating egg salad."

Dana double-checks the address Ms. Callus gave us and points ahead. "What do you think Ms. Callus's house will look like?"

"Like her office but with a fridge and a bed. Though she might not have a bed. She might sleep hanging upside down from the rafters. I also think it will be very, very brown," I say, indicating Dana's Saint Margaret's uniform.

"I wonder if she's a carpet or hardwood-floor type

of person? Curtains or blinds? Midcentury coolness or Scandi chic? Ooh, this is it."

We stop in front of a large gray house that has a pond with a statue of a lady overlooking it.

"Is that Ms. Callus?" Dana asks as she nears the six-foot-high block of marble.

"I didn't know you could get statues made of yourself," I say. "Where would you even order this?"

Dana peers closely at the face of the statue and then back at me. "It's actually a really good likeness."

I take the keys from my pocket as a crew of barking dogs erupts on the road. Dana and I both turn to see a flustered-looking man being pulled left and right by six puppies.

"Good afternoon, Hyacinth."

Hyacinth? I mentally roll my eyes. Such a typical old-lady name.

"Aww, look at your little cutie patooties," I say as the dogs snuffle closer.

A teddy-faced Shiba Inu takes one look at me and bares its teeth. Now, I don't know if you've ever seen an angry Shiba Inu before, but it's really unsettling. Like seeing a baby koala lose its temper.

"Sorry," the dog walker says as he tries to pull the irritated pup away. "I've never known her to growl at you before." He looks back up and nods at Dana. "Hello there. You must be Hyacinth's granddaughter."

"Granddaughter?" I laugh. "Don't be silly. She's seven weeks older than me."

Dana stares at me and widens her eyes.

I hesitate. "Oh . . . yes, of course. This is my . . . uh . . ." The lie gets trapped in my throat like a tough old brussels sprout. "Granddaughter," I manage eventually. "The daughter of my daughter. Or the daughter of my son. Who knows. Ha, ha." I reach over and pat Dana on the head in a grandmotherly way. "Yes, I have a granddaughter. It's true and not a lie at all."

The Shiba Inu is still chucking out bad vibes, growling at me and looking ready to pounce.

"Come on, *Grandmother*," Dana orders as she opens the front door and pulls me into the house. "Let's go inside and you can tell me stories about the olden days."

As the door slams shut behind us, I exhale, relieved.

"That dog definitely knew your secret," Dana says.

"The dog knew I cheated on the times tables quiz?"

"No, that you're not really who you appear to be."

I roll up my sleeves, expecting to see a swathe of red bumps from lying. There's nothing. "Phew. Now what?"

"Well, I don't know what galaxy you're in," Dana says, "but I'm ready for some serious snooping."

The pungent smell of potpourri hits us as we walk through the hallway, which is lined with photographs of a youthful-looking Ms. Callus.

"So weird to see her smiling," Dana muses.

I cock an eyebrow at a photo of Ms. Callus on a beach in a gold caftan. She's wearing sandals and her toes are on full display. "I don't like seeing teachers on vacation. It's like seeing your parents kiss."

We carry on through to the living room, which looks as if a greenhouse has exploded in it. The walls are a flowery lilac and pink, the carpet a pale swirly yellow, and every piece of furniture is covered in prints of little birds.

"Oh," I say, "it's very . . ."

"Springlike?" Dana tries.

"Yes. And . . ."

"Fresh?"

"Hmm. I was expecting it to be browner, but I guess she does wear a lot of pastels to school."

There are several large gilt-framed paintings on the wall, all of our principal.

"You've got to admire this level of self-confidence," Dana says. "And look up."

I glance up obediently. Even the ceiling is covered in intricate murals of Ms. Callus.

"Teaching does seem to attract narcissists," Dana observes.

I stand by a giant painting of Ms. Callus dressed as Marie Antoinette and holding a baguette. "Did I miss the part where we found out Ms. Callus was a member of the French aristocracy?" I sit on the plush sofa and pop my old-lady feet up on the glass coffee table, avoiding a large vase of flowers and an ancient-looking chess set. "I'm surprised she lives somewhere so fancy. I thought teachers were poor."

Dana strokes the pink velvety cushions thoughtfully. "It smells of extreme wealth in here. Perhaps she dabbles in the stock market or was an early investor in cryptocurrencies. I must talk business with her when this is all over." Dana's watch beeps and she lifts a finger. "Incoming notification. Ooh, AZ8 has announced the title!"

I gasp and spring over to read the video comeback title: "Hot Feet." We look at each other and start jumping up and down until something snaps in my left side.

"Ouch," I cry, grasping the spot where the pain is.

"You really *are* like my grandmother," says Dana.

"I keep getting all these weird aches and pains. Do you think it's something to do with the magic?"

"It's probably more to do with you being two hundred

years old. Or a lack of vitamin C." She laughs. "Can you imagine Ms. Callus eating a kiwi or Kakadu plum?"

"No. I've never seen her eat anything."

"Me neither. On that subject, let's get some snacks."

We stroll back through the hallway, pausing to study a series of black-and-white photographs of Ms. Callus lying in a field of tulips, smelling roses and blowing dandelion seeds at the camera.

"Weird, weird, weird," I say.

The kitchen isn't floral, but brown—so very, very brown. Cabinets, counters, floor, ceiling, everything!

"Ah," I mutter. "Now this is more how I imagined her place would look. Right, Dana? Dana?" I panic. "Where are you?"

"Over here," she calls, waving from a few feet in front of me.

I sigh with relief. "Phew. With your uniform you totally blended in for a second. I feel lightheaded; I need to eat something."

We fling open the mahogany cupboard doors to find the insides stacked three deep with jars. "Chunky Monkey peanut butter, my favorite."

We make sandwiches and head back to the living room, where I sweep the chess set to one side to make room on the coffee table.

"Aaahhh," I yawn, still not used to the high soaring voice that comes out of me.

Dana's watch beeps several times. "I set up a group chat with Ms. Callus," she explains. "I've got an old phone somewhere at home. I'll bring it to school for you tomorrow. That way we can keep in touch throughout the day about the whole switching back into your own body thing."

"Good idea." I take a huge chewy mouthful of my sandwich and try to ignore the way my teeth move with each bite. At what age do people start wearing dentures anyway?

"Can I have a look at the messages?" I grab Dana's phone and open up the Body Swappers Anonymous group chat.

First message:

> **Ms. Callus:** Is this cat supposed to smell like fish?

Second message:

> **Ms. Callus:** A young man called Jesse lives here; he reminds me of someone I expelled eight years ago.

Third message:

> **Ms. Callus:** Please do not disturb my chessboard. I have been playing that game with myself for the past seventeen months.

Whoops.

"Skylar," Dana says, "aren't you curious how Ms. Callus is doing at your home with your family?"

I think it over for all of three seconds. "Nope." Because, really, I'm still so angry at my parents for their completely over-the-top reaction to me wanting to dedicate my life to AZ8. "I only care about AZ8. Five minutes to go."

We both turn to the wall opposite the sofa expecting a giant screen; however, there's only a bookshelf, which is filled with books and, you've guessed it, more beauty shots of Ms. Callus.

"That's odd." I look around—there's no sign of a TV in here. I check the kitchen and then the bedroom upstairs, that has no TV but a life-size painting of Ms. Callus sitting on top of an elephant while wearing a yellow polka-dot bikini, which is unkind to both elephants and my eyes.

By the time I hobble back downstairs, Dana is in

full-blown panic mode. "She doesn't have a TV!" she screams. "Ninety-six point four percent of British households have at least one TV."

It's so disappointing because while we don't mind watching AZ8 on our phones, something like a video comeback really deserves a big screen, especially with a title as promising as "Hot Feet."

We send Ms. Callus an urgent message:

> **Me:** TV location?

After what seems like a lifetime of her typing, a reply comes through:

> **Ms. Callus:** Television? Why not indulge yourself with a spot of homework instead?

I growl in frustration and type back:

> **Me:** We want to watch the news. To catch up on important global events.

She sends back a smiley face.

"Dana, did you teach Ms. Callus how to use emojis?"

Then another message:

> **Ms. Callus:** There's an enthralling documentary exploring the greatest rail journeys of Britain. I think you would both enjoy it. The television set is in the basement.

We find a door that opens onto a dark, dingy staircase.

"I'm not sure about this," I say. "Basements are eerie. If this was a horror movie, there would definitely be some kind of creepy zombie down there."

"No, in horror movies it's upstairs where the creepy zombie hides. Look, we're running out of time and I'm not prepared to miss the opening seconds of 'Hot Feet.' What would Woojin do when faced with a dark, scary basement in a strange floral house?"

I think about it for a moment. "He would blow a kiss and backflip down these stairs."

"Exactly. Let's go."

We hold hands and bravely head down. I admit that once the lights are on, it's not that scary at all, unless you're scared of millions of old box files with labels like CURRICULUM 2001 and EXPULSIONS 1988. Which I am. There's also a dusty old sofa but no obvious screen.

"Now, if I were a piece of televisual equipment, where would I be?" Dana wonders.

"Aha!" I find it hidden on a shelf on the far wall. It's old and bulky and a little part of me expects the picture to be black-and-white. Thank goodness I'm wrong.

Dana manages to get YouTube on it by doing something clever with her phone, and the words *Hot Feet* appear in bright pink letters. Woojin's smiling face fills the screen as the video begins.

"He's got blue hair!" I cry.

Jungwon looks so cool in a furry bucket hat; Garam stuns in a gold suit; Haru's dance break is awe-inspiring; Tae's dimples are popping; when Yujun sings high notes he doesn't sound like a human at all but an angel; and of course Dig-D and Dig-C both look great in the background. There's also the most amazing dance routine I have ever seen in my life to go with the soul-shatteringly beautiful lyrics of *"Hot Feet, don't stop; hot feet, do the bop. Hot feet, go whippety-whop, and I love you."*

"Hot Feet" is without doubt AZ8's best-ever song and best-ever video. Once it's over, we turn to each other, ready to unpack every little detail. We usually do a detailed debrief before watching the video another eight times, each time focusing on the brilliance of a specific member. But then something weird happens: Woojin pops back on the screen.

"Hey, Glows." He points at the camera, and it's like he's pointing right at us.

"Yes?" we reply as we shuffle closer.

"AZ8 wants to know: How hot are your feet?"

Dana gasps. "Oh my gosh, he's talking to us!"

I shush her.

Woojin continues. "We're giving away fifty pairs of tickets to our sold-out show in London this Saturday. To win, upload a video of yourself doing the 'Hot Feet' dance by six p.m. tomorrow. Good luck, and don't forget to sparkle like confetti."

Dana's mouth drops open. "What on the third planet in the solar system is going on? I think I'm going to faint. Or cry. Or throw up. I need to lie down." She flops on the sofa and closes her eyes.

"Tickets to the show," I say. "Whoa. That would be amazing."

Dana bounces back up and grabs me by the shoulders. "This is it, Skylar. Your chance to show the world your skills."

"Me?"

She nods. "You're one of the greatest undiscovered dancers of our time."

"I love to dance, yes, but I'm not that great."

"What are you talking about? Some of your online dance videos have literally twenty-seven views."

"Yeah, but aren't most of those views you?"

"I'm your biggest fan."

"My only fan," I point out.

"Only because you keep your talent hidden," she argues.

It's true that while I post the occasional video of myself dancing online, I don't tell anyone about it.

"This is your moment to show the world how amazing you are."

"Aw." I make a hand heart. "Thanks, Dana. But this is like a real competition."

"And you're a real dancer."

"I'm also an old lady till 2:22 tomorrow."

She shrugs. "What difference does it make? You're still Skylar under all that old-lady skin."

"I can barely walk at a normal speed, never mind do a cartwheel while looking cute. Plus, it's impossible to get noticed online. Look." I point to the screen, where forty-four #HotFeet videos have already been uploaded. I click on the first one. How have people learned the dance so quickly? They're good too. "I can't compete with this. No way. I'm more of a dance-in-secret kind of person."

"You can at least try," Dana says.

I stand up straighter and attempt to mimic Woojin's spin and high kick from the video. I can do it, though it feels a little slower in this body—a little creakier too.

"Ouch," I say as my hip starts to give out on the drop. "Can you imagine if I entered as Ms. Callus?" I laugh. "That would be so crazy."

Dana gasps. "That's an Einstein idea."

"No, it's a terrible idea."

"You'd stand out like a liquid among gases."

I shake my head. "No way." I sit back down carefully, holding my sore hip. "This body is super uncomfortable by the way, so as nice as all this freedom is, I can't wait to be back in my own body tomorrow. Then *maybe* we can think about entering this challenge."

Dana's cheeks flush a little.

"What?" I ask suspiciously. "I *am* going to swap back into my own body at 2:22 tomorrow, right? That's what you said. Twenty-four hours of having my very misguided wish come true and then everything will switch back to normal."

Dana gives me her biggest grin and says, "Of course. When have I ever been wrong about anything?"

5
WALKING IN ANOTHER PERSON'S HEELS

I wake up to a phone ringing.

Bringggg-bringggg.

As in an actual phone, like it's connected to a wall and everything.

Though there's no way I'm getting up. Every muscle in my body hurts.

Bringggg-bringggg.

My eyes are stuck together. Ugh.

Bringggg-bringggg.

I blindly stick my hand out and grope around, knocking something on the bedside table while trying to grab the handset.

Bringggg-bri—

"What?" I croak.

"You're late," a voice, which sounds distinctively like my own, fires back.

"Huh?" I sit up in bed and the creaking in my back combined with the sea of floral duvet surrounding me brings it all flooding back. The lightning. The body swap. Woojin's blue hair. It was all real.

"It's half past six," Ms. Callus barks. "A principal should arrive at school no later than the crack of dawn."

"I . . . I . . . I don't feel so well, Ms. Callus. Maybe the lightning hurt me worse than I realized. My whole body aches."

"Little Miss Skylar, I am of an advanced age. Every day there are aches, pain, suffering. A broken hip here, a glass eye there, but I don't let it stop me. You know why?"

"Because you like pain?"

"No. Because I am a responsible adult and my life is hard. I can't just get my mommy to call in sick for me when I have a little boo-boo. Now, I must run; I heard there's Nutella and toast at Bright and Brainy Breakfast Club—what a treat! You children really are spoiled. Adieu, adieu."

Right, I need to get ready. OK, I can do this.

I open the wardrobe, which is filled with twinsets

in every color, many of them covered with some kind of floral pattern. The shoes all have heels, and there are loads of flowing silk scarves I'm not quite sure how to rock. I hate it all but eventually decide on a pale green skirt, pale yellow blouse, and pale pink cardigan. I also tie a pale gray scarf around my neck. I've never seen Ms. Callus wear this particular combo, but she should because it looks pretty stunning. I accessorize with a hairpin, brooch, earrings, four necklaces, seven rings, and an ankle bracelet. The watch is still stuck at 2:22 so I don't bother putting it on.

"Uniform policy?" I say as I look my stylish self over in the mirror. "Why, I *am* the uniform policy." I do a little spin and a dignified backward shuffle, super pleased with myself.

Despite sleeping on it, the helmet hair is still in place, though leaning a little to the right. What next? Ah yes, makeup. Bit of blush here, some lipstick there, eyeliner—yes, drawing around your eyes with a big black pencil is a thing . . . Weird. Still, OK. Done.

I take another quick peek in the dressing-table mirror.

"Whoa, you make old look awesome."

I take the liberty of ordering a taxi, and man, do I feel like an absolute superstar in the back of the Prius, speeding past bus stops packed with rowdy kids and getting dropped off right in front of the school gates.

I spot my friend Anthony by the reception desk. "Morning, my fellow Glow," I shout, because this is how we fans like to greet one another. But he doesn't shout back or flick me a finger heart; instead he looks really confused and almost frightened. Then I remember. Yikes, I'm the enemy; I'm Ms. Callus.

As a sixth grader no one cares about, I'm used to walking around school unnoticed, but now I can't take a step without producing some sort of reaction. People hush as I approach, gum is swallowed, earbuds are pulled, candy wrappers are stuffed into pockets.

"Good morning, Ms. Callus," the students grovel.

A group of eighth graders heads toward me and I do a little swerve to the right to see if they change course. They do. I swerve to the left. They switch back. Each time I change direction they do as well. Left, right, left. Hilarious. Then when I turn around and start walking backward, straight toward them, they scatter and apologize like it's *their* fault.

I head down the side of the science block, which is usually a no-go area for sixth graders, and a plume of sweet-smelling strawberry smoke hits me.

"Boo!" I shout, and a gang of ninth graders jumps

out of their skin. Rayan Khan, the most feared boy in school, drops something and kicks it away.

"What was that?" I bellow.

For a moment, I think Rayan is going to bite back. After all, he's the same boy who once held the design teacher out of a top-floor window by one leg. Or at least that's what *I* heard.

I bend over with some difficulty and grab the offending item. A vape. Busted.

"Detention!" I shout. "All of you. All week."

"No, please," they cry.

"Actually, make that ALL TERM."

"We're sorry, please, no," they beg in vain.

This is fun. I laugh all the way to *my* office, where I sit in the big green chair behind the giant desk and close my eyes. I've learned to walk in Ms. Callus's shoes all right, and apart from a few blisters, this life is easier than the dance break in AZ8's "Smoother Than Silky Silk."

Knock-knock. I jump up from the chair as the school secretary, Mr. Idle, marches in.

"Good morning," I say quickly.

When you're one minute late for school, it's Mr. Idle who decides if you get marked in on time or not, so you must always be nice to him.

He slams a mug down on the desk. "Your coffee. I'm the only one getting the milk at the moment. What am I? A cow? Since when was that part of *my* job?"

"Ooh, coffee," I say brightly. "You know how we adults can't function without it. Frothy coffee, my favorite tasty drink." I take a sip. "Eww. Ugh. Yuck."

He stares at me. "What's happened to your face?" he asks curiously.

My face? Is the magic wearing off? I touch my papery skin . . . No, still old.

"You look more . . . *colorful* than usual." Mr. Idle narrows his eyes. "Anyway, shall we start?"

"Start with the busywork? Yes, yes." I turn to the computer and type my username: SkylarSmith and password: W00JIN4EVA. Declined. Yikes.

Mr. Idle taps his foot. "Is there a problem, Ms. Callus?"

"Uh, I think my computer is broken. I can't seem to log in." I try again, this time typing in username: HyacinthCallus and taking a guess at password: SHAKESPEARE4EVA. Declined, yet again.

Mr. Idle huffs and leans over me. "Here, let me do it." He types so fast I don't get to see, but at least I'm logged in. "I've loaded your schedule for today onto the computer. Now, do you need me for anything else?" he asks.

"I'd love a KitKat and a banana milk."

He screws up his face. "What do you think I am? Your secretary?"

"Uh, aren't you?"

He tuts as he stomps out of the office.

I quickly learn that being a principal is mostly saying "Oh right, I'll make sure that doesn't happen again" and nodding a lot. I do it with a parent who comes in to talk to me about how their "spirited" child got called disruptive, again with another parent who complains their kid turned green after falling in the science garden pond, and again with the custodian who tells me he found three squirrels in one of the gym changing rooms.

Two minutes after the bell for lunch rings, Mr. Idle calls me. "Ms. Callus, there's a sixth-grade child out here who says she needs to see you; she says it's desperate."

As I put the phone down, Ms. Callus bursts in looking . . . well, like me, but also so very *not* like me.

"What are you wearing?" Shined shoes, non-holey socks, a crisply ironed uniform and . . . *argh*. "What have you done to my hair?" I ask, horrified.

She twirls a pigtail. "Cute, don't you think?"

"You've given me doo-doo braids," I say angrily.

"That's how my mom used to do my hair when I was in preschool."

"Enjoyed playing with makeup, did you?" she retorts. "You look like Coco the Clown."

"I'm eleven years old; I don't know how to do makeup."

"Did you find the morning very tough?" Ms. Callus asks in a babyish voice.

"No," I snap back. "It was easy. Just as I knew it would be."

"Not as easy as *my* morning. Goodness, being eleven is like being on vacation."

"Yeah, if your vacation included double math. How was it, by the way?"

"Fantastic fun. I love learning about the division of fractions. I must say, being a child today is easier than it's ever been before. Not like in my day when we were—"

"Up chimneys?" I suggest. "Down coal mines? Playing in bomb craters? Walking with dinosaurs?" I shuffle some papers on the desk, because I think shuffling papers is another big part of the job. Then I wait a few moments before asking, "Do you think my parents suspected anything?"

"They hardly noticed me. Your mother was completely absorbed by something called *Love at the*

Cupcake Café, and your father was too busy trying to cultivate a spider plant."

"Oh." Well, that's rude. "What about Nana? There's no way she didn't notice I was different, that I was suddenly way less cool."

Ms. Callus chuckles. "Oh, Nana is delightful. I stayed up late with her eating bacon-and-bean burritos while she regaled me with tales of her exciting childhood."

"That's good," I say through gritted teeth.

How can no one have noticed that I was an entirely different person? What kind of family are they anyway?!

Ms. Callus smiles smugly.

"Are you ready for lunch?" I ask maliciously. "It's Thai Tofu Tuesday."

She shivers.

"What's wrong?" I smirk. "Not in the mood for a mango-and-bean-curd omelet today? I'm so glad I'm an adult who can order in pizza. It's a good thing my life is this easy. Now, I'd better be off."

"Where are you going?" Ms. Callus cries as she jumps lithely into my path.

"To the staff room, of course. Did you really think I would pass on this once-in-a-girlhood opportunity to go inside the room of secrets?"

"A principal doesn't eat in the staff room. It makes the other teachers act strangely."

"The other teachers *are* strange." I mull it over. "Hang on, don't you all hang out here together on the weekends and stuff?"

"No. Or they might, but they don't invite me." She pouts sadly. "I have lunch in here, alone."

"Well, I'm not eating alone." I head to the door.

"They don't like you," Ms. Callus calls as I leave. "You're the principal—they don't want to be your friend."

I stand outside the place no student has gone before and take a deep breath. Once I pass over this threshold, I'm going to see things no young eyes should ever see and, who knows, it may scar me for life. But I'm ready.

Inside, it's nicer than I imagined. Big, airy, and very quiet. A few teachers are grading at tables, some are sleeping, and Coach Cathy is in the middle pumping up basketballs and downing a protein shake.

"Hey, everyone," I say.

Nothing.

"So, uh, how did everyone's lessons go this morning? Who was great, who was bad, who'd you shout at?"

Another awkward silence.

"Uh, anyone want to talk about K-pop bands?" A few

teachers exchange looks. "No? No one? Cool. I'll start. I'm a Glow, but who does everyone stan here?"

Mr. Antwi, the woodworking teacher, flips over a coffee table to check the strength of the legs and then asks, "Stan? Is he that chatty boy in eighth grade?"

"No," I say. "*Stan*. It means you're appropriately obsessed with something."

Mr. Antwi shakes his head. "I don't stan any pop bands."

I sigh inwardly. Don't these teachers know anything?

"Stan is bigger than bands," I explain. "You can stan lesser things. For example, Coach Cathy stans Arsenal Soccer Club; Ms. Barnard stans Picasso; and you, Mr. Antwi, you stan destruction and rebuilding."

"It's true," he admits as he snaps a leg off the table. "I love it."

"People, people," I say as I encourage them to gather around. "K-pop is where it's at. If you want to reach us— uh, I mean, reach the students, it helps to understand what they're into, so you know what's important in their lives and you don't do anything stupid, like banning AZ8 for a week."

"I hear you, sister," Mr. Keen shouts from behind a cloud of fragrant beard spray. "That's why the students see me more like their best friend than their computing teacher."

The German teacher, Herr Schneider, raises his tiny hand and says something I don't understand, which isn't unusual because for some reason he chooses to only speak in German.

"Sorry, what did you say over there?" I ask.

Mr. Antwi does some top-notch translation, then says, "He's a Flossy."

I gasp. "No way."

A Flossy, in case you don't know, is someone who's a fan of the Korean all-girl supergroup White Teeth.

Herr Schneider connects his phone to the staff room speaker and puts on White Teeth's hit single "You Can Smile but You Can't Hide."

"I don't get it," Mr. Ben, a tall, willowy man who teaches piano, moans. "You can't even understand what they're saying."

I roll my eyes. "So what? We don't understand what Shakespeare is saying half the time either. Right, everyone up."

And amazingly, because I'm the principal, every last one of them leaves their microwaved fish curries and stands up.

"Let's learn a dance routine. It goes like this: *To the left, to the right, now make your hips shine bright. To the front, to the back, now give your butt a smack.*"

Herr Schneider nails it like the dance monster he is, and then everyone joins in. Mr. Ben is really feeling it, eyes closed, arms waving as if he's trying to stop a runaway train, while Mr. Keen has gone for a more hip-thrusting, aggressive finger-pointing approach.

I'm not usually a huge fan of White Teeth, but it feels so good to dance, especially after the stress of yesterday.

"You're really good," Coach Cathy calls over to me as she improvises a particularly athletic twirl.

"Thanks," I yell back, "you too."

Ms. Barnard takes the paintbrushes from her hair and starts drumming them against the wall while wriggling her butt, and I jump up on a coffee table and clap along. "Ms. Barnard, you've got rhythm for days. Whoop-whoop!"

Technically, some of the teachers are really struggling, especially when it comes to telling their left from their right, their hand from their foot, their twerk from their tango, but they're enjoying themselves so much it doesn't matter; the whole thing is infectiously fun.

"Mr. Antwi, it'll be easier to dance if you put down the saw," I advise.

I turn the music up, but just as we're really getting into it, the bell rings.

"Aw, lunch is always too short," I moan as the teachers

gather their things and down the last of their coffees.

Such a shame. I was really enjoying myself.

"It's so nice to finally meet you," Coach Cathy says.

I'm puzzled. "Meet me? Um, don't we work together?"

"Yes, but you've never spoken to me before. You've never spoken to any of us."

"Actually," Mr. Antwi huffs, "you did shout at me once."

"Me too," says Ms. Barnard as she wipes sweat from her forehead. "You once screamed at me in front of my seventh-grade art class for having dirty paint pots."

"That's horrible," I say. "No wonder you all looked so shocked when I came in here."

Mr. Ben nods. "We were scared you were coming in to tell us off."

Why is Ms. Callus like this? It's one thing to have students scared of you, but having your own teachers cowering in fear seems a little excessive.

"I'm sorry," I say on her behalf.

"Dudette," Mr. Keen drawls. "Don't sweat it."

"Yeah," Mr. Antwi agrees. "We know you have a stressful job."

Coach Cathy smiles and says, "Perhaps you'll come back and have lunch with us again?"

"Really?" I grin. "Cool, that would be great."

And just like that, I've made Ms. Callus some friends.

6
AVOCADO

I'm still buzzing when I get back to Ms. Callus's office, so I burn off some energy by dancing to a phenomenal playlist called "AZ8: The Remixes Remixed." I listen through headphones, though every time I do something loud like a bit of Billy Bouncing or krumping, Mr. Idle pops through and makes a loaded comment about noisy workplaces leading to high incidences of staff absence.

In the end I give up and sit sulkily behind the massive desk, sharpening pencils and touching up my makeup—boring—waiting as the clock slowly creeps closer to 2:22 when I can finally get my body back. At two p.m. I put out a call on the announcement system for Dana and Ms. Callus.

"I can't believe you summoned me like this," Dana yells as she storms in. "I was in a student council meeting. We had already solved seventy-seven point seven percent of the world's problems. Side note, you look great." She makes a heart sign with her hands. "I love this whole orange blush thing you've got going on."

"You don't think it's too Halloweeny?"

"Yes, I do, and it's fabulous. Anyway, how are you feeling? Ready to be young again?"

"Yes, because as much as I've loved the wild spending on Ms. Callus's school credit card, unlimited screen time, and the simple joy of not washing up a single thing, I'm really bored and my hip hurts."

"So, what you're saying is, now you've walked in Ms. Callus's shoes you understand that being old and in charge isn't all fun and games?"

I think about it for a moment, and yes, it's true. "Whoa. I've been taught a lesson on empathy and not even noticed it was happening. I do have one question, though."

"Is it about how to recycle grocery bags? Because I've already explained you can only do that at the big supermarkets."

"No, it's about Ms. Callus. Like, if your old movie theory is right, surely Ms. Callus *also* needs to have learned something about being me in order for the swap to work. Right?"

"Yes, and she has. I saw her in the hall earlier and she has the biggest zit in the world right now. She's actually thinking of hiring a school dermatologist. If that's not empathy, I don't know what is."

Just then Dana's watch pings with the unmistakable sound of an AZ8 alert. She gets out her phone.

"Oh my . . . oh my. AZ8 are going live on *Live-Right-Now*. I bet they want to remind everyone of the 'Hot Feet' challenge. And by everyone, I'm obviously talking about you."

"Hmm," I say, as I perch on the desk next to Dana. "I'm still not sure about entering."

"Why not?"

"I told you—I'm not good enough, and—Whoa, look how pretty Tae is today."

Dana squeals. "He looks so sweet in his yellow T-shirt, like a chick on Easter Sunday."

Garam and Yujun appear on the screen next.

"Is Garam reading poetry? Aw, he's so clever and sensitive."

I'm half aware of someone coming into the office and talking, but there's no way I can peel my eyes from the beautiful scene of AZ8 sitting in a bare room and having a conversation in a language I don't know. It's riveting.

"Hello?" Ms. Callus sings at the top of her voice.

"Shh!" we fire back.

She peers over our shoulders and sniffs. "Is this them? The AZY9 boys?"

"AZ8," I correct, looking up and doing a double take. It's still so weird seeing my face on her face, if that makes sense, and yes, that is indeed a rather large chin zit.

"Why are you staring at me like that?" Ms. Callus snaps, lifting a notepad and holding it self-consciously in front of her.

"Because you have my face!" I retort.

She scoffs and removes the pad, looking at the screen again. "Why, these young hoodlums aren't even speaking in English!"

"Of course not, they're Korean." I roll my eyes at her. "We have to wait for the translation. For now, we watch and try to guess what they're talking about."

Tae holds an avocado toward the camera and makes a tutting noise.

"What are all these little hearts at the bottom about?" Ms. Callus asks.

"That shows the number of people watching and sending their virtual love."

Ms. Callus is shocked. "You mean to tell me there

are three point two million people across the world watching a tattooed urchin babble on about avocado?"

"Yes," I say, "and he's not an urchin; he's an angel."

Dana grins. "Avocados are a great source of potassium, but Tae's right—they are kind of disgusting."

The other band members come into shot. Cue more screaming. Ms. Callus winces and puts her fingers in her ears.

We continue watching the live feed, which is wonderful but difficult to enjoy with Ms. Callus constantly counting down the minutes to 2:22 beside us. Then the boys sign off and we have over ten minutes left, enough time to watch "Hot Feet" again. And again. And ag—

"Enough!" Ms. Callus shouts. "I don't understand any of this."

"How can you not love it?" Dana asks. "Or are you pretending not to love it because they're a boy band?"

"Yeah." I put my hands on my creaking hips. "If there's one thing that really gets my back up, it's people not giving AZ8's music a chance just because they happen to be boys and in a band."

Ms. Callus snatches Dana's phone and peers closely at the screen. "There are so many of them. How are you supposed to know all their names?"

The thing is, no one ever asks a teacher how they

know the names of all the kids in their class, or a soccer fan how they know the names of every player on their team, or a parent how they know the names of their children. But if you know the names of a few boy band members, it's somehow weird.

"I know AZ8 by their stage names, nicknames, *and* full Korean names," I say proudly.

Dana raises her hand. "I can write their names in Hangul."

"Oh wow!" I laugh, impressed. "Well, I can't do that. I've only just mastered cursive handwriting, never mind Korean!"

Ms. Callus frowns at the video. She's going to give me premature wrinkles if she keeps doing that. "But they all look the same. Same clothes. Same multicolored hairstyles. Same pose."

"Listen carefully," I say to her. "In birth order: Jungwon, Tae, Yujun, Garam, Haru, Dig-D, Dig-C, and Woojin, also known as the diamond *maknae*. I can recognize them by their shoulder width, moles, or forehead alone."

Ms. Callus groans. "And you?" she says, waving the phone in Dana's direction. "You're one of the highest-achieving sixth graders we've ever had. Surely you don't spend all your time studying this ridiculous boy band?"

Dana's eyes widen and she whispers, "I can recognize them by their shadows."

Ms. Callus throws up her hands in frustration and clears her throat. "Right. Enough of this nonsense. It's 2:17."

We sit across from each other and stare as we wait for the swap to be reversed. I hope it won't be as scary as it was yesterday.

"Did you two have fun as each other?" Dana asks. "OK, I guess *fun* isn't the right word. But you've both definitely learned a lot. Skylar, you're now empathetic toward older adults with cartilage erosion; Ms. Callus, you're now empathetic toward adolescents with overactive oil glands."

"What time is it?" I ask impatiently.

Dana checks. "It's 2:20."

My nerves begin to frazzle. "What time is it *now*?"

"Still 2:20," Dana says.

We wait.

Another minute ticks by, and 2:21 comes and goes. As does 2:22, 2:23, and then 2:24, and, to be honest, I'm getting stressed about the lack of magical goings-on as well as feeling very awkward about having this much eye contact with Ms. Callus, who, in case you've forgotten, has my face.

It's now 2:30.

Why is nothing happening? This is bad. This is very, very bad.

"Dana, are you sure we don't need the storm and lightning?" I ask.

She scrunches up her nose. "I don't *think* so. Maybe your reasons for empathizing with each other weren't deep enough. I mean, zits and aching hips . . . What else have you learned?"

Ms. Callus and I shrug.

"Come on, dig deep. Sit closer," Dana instructs. "And perhaps hold hands."

We sit closer and take each other by the hand and, I must say, holding my own hand is one of the weirdest things I have ever had to do. Ms. Callus then crosses her legs, which looks like a super awkward way to sit, and says, "Yes, I've learned that sixth-grade students have plenty of free time, and a few more hours of homework wouldn't go amiss."

I gasp in horror. Is she seriously saying that after twenty-four hours she still can't see how tough a young person's life is compared with hers? And to think I was feeling sorry for her with her achy bones.

"Well, in that case," I start, "I've learned that being a principal involves absolutely no teaching at all. In fact, it involves nothing really. Just lots of sitting around and nodding at people. Also, you get paid way too much money to do that."

"I've learned," Ms. Callus continues, her voice growing angry, "that your handwriting is atrocious."

"I've learned that even though nuts are banned at Saint Margaret's, you have an entire drawer full of them."

"I've learned—"

"Stop!" Dana shouts. "No wonder this isn't working. Neither of you have learned anything of importance."

"I've learned the meaning of the word *empathy*!" I shout back.

"Not enough," said Dana.

It's now 2:38.

"We're not going to switch back, are we?" I ask despairingly. "This is it. I'm trapped forever."

Dana shakes her head. "That's not how it works, Skylar. In every single movie and book with a body swap, there's a very clear end point. Though maybe I jumped to the wrong conclusion with the whole twenty-four hours thing. Perhaps it's more of a whole-school-week thing, like Monday to Friday."

"I'm going to be stuck like this till Friday?" I wail. Is she crazy? "I can't face a Wednesday, Thursday, and Friday in this old sack of bones."

I rest my big helmet head against the desk. This is awful. This is worse than being grounded, than getting detention, than having to attend math tutoring. I can't hold it in any longer; I start to cry.

When I look up to take a tissue from Dana, I spot a smirk flash across Ms. Callus's face. "Why are you so happy about this?" I shriek. Yes, I actually shriek at my principal because that's how wound up I am.

She wobbles her head from side to side. "My dear child, when you get to my age—"

"Which right now is eleven."

"No, I am of course speaking of my *real* age, which is seventy-one. A few days is nothing in the grand scheme of things. Also, if I'm being completely honest, I'm quite tickled by the idea of extending my vacation on the island of youth for a few more days."

"*Vacation?*" I echo, aghast.

"And the best part is," she adds, completely ignoring me, "I can still govern in disguise. What better way to find out if staff and students are up to scratch than by watching them covertly, like a glamorous war spy."

"You're enjoying this," I grumble. "You're on the wrong side of history, lady."

Ms. Callus stands up with ease, rather than effort and creaks like I do now, and flicks a pigtail over her shoulder. "Ooh, look, it's almost dismissal time; that means I can join my new buddies in After-School Academics Club. See you at 2:22 on Friday. Don't work too hard." And with a little flourish of a wave, she leaves.

"At least you get out of doing your math test," Dana says after a moment of silence.

"How could you make this mistake?" I cry.

"Because I don't know everything."

"Yes, you do. You're a genius. That's the exact definition of it."

"That's a very common miscon—"

"Stop!" I yell. I am so furious with her right now. I'm going to be stuck as an old lady for a whole week of my life because my best friend got it wrong.

"Please, don't get stressed, Skylar. I really think—"

Dana flinches as I slam my hands on the desk. "You've done enough thinking for one day. Now, if you'll excuse me, I have work to do."

Dana's face falls, then she says to the ground, "Fine, I'll leave you alone."

I try my very best not to watch as she shuffles miserably to the door. I should say something—I know I'm not being fair—but I'm too angry right now. Dana shuts the door quietly behind her, leaving me to read a document titled *Behave, Behave, Behave—Why Youth Must Behave*.

7
CALL AN AMBULANCE

I pop into the shops on the way home to stock up on essentials. Bread, milk, bananas, a microwavable chicken curry, and a churros machine. Anything to try and cheer myself up after the worst Tuesday on record. A day where I have realized the following:

1. I'm trapped as Ms. Callus till Friday, or possibly till death.

2. Shouting at my bestie and slamming my hands on a hard wooden desk makes me feel sad.

3. Slamming my hands on a hard wooden desk bruises them.

I sit on Ms. Callus's large flowery sofa and eat my

chicken curry, which is nowhere near as nice as the ones Nana makes every Tuesday. After I finish, I putter about for a bit, unsure of what to do with myself. I play chess, but it's as boring as when grown-ups talk about parking spots. I think I have another point for the list:

4. Playing board games without your family, even if your mom cheats, your dad drops crumbs on the board, and your brother always wins, is no fun.

The doorbell rings and I hear a voice. "Skylar? Skylar? Open up."

I creep to the front door to see Dana's fingers wagging through the letter box.

"What do you want?" I ask grumpily. Because as glad as I am to hear a friendly voice, I'm still annoyed about her making such a big mistake today.

"Please, open the door."

I crack it a little to check that the dog walker and his crazed pooches aren't close. "What are you doing here?" I try to ask in my scary principal voice, but it comes out a little whiny.

"What do you think I'm doing here?"

"I don't know," I say snootily. "That's why I asked."

Dana holds up a party-size box of matcha mochi doughnuts. "I bought too many, and you know how I feel about food waste."

I do know how she feels about food waste as I've recently listened to her podcast, *Dana Explains Food Waste*. I also know she's more than capable of finishing a party-size box of matcha mochi doughnuts on her own.

She gives me a sad half smile and I feel all soft, because none of this is really her fault. She was only trying to help. I open the door wide and throw my arms around her. "Sorry for shouting at you earlier."

Dana shrugs. "It's OK. It was a high-stress situation; everyone's cortisol was through the roof. Here, I've brought you something to help with your extended period of adulting." She rummages in her backpack and takes out a mug with Woojin's beautiful face on it. "It's a heat mug, so when you make a hot drink, he gets freckles."

I hold the mug against my heart. "This is the most thoughtful gift anyone has ever given me. Thank you, Dana."

We sit side by side on the sofa and share the doughnuts, before moving on to some chips and then a bag of fruit chews.

"Did you notice how Ms. Callus wasn't that bothered when we couldn't swap back today?" I ask.

"Hmm, yeah. She seems to be enjoying herself."

"Is she acing all my work for me?"

Dana laughs. "At a cost."

I frown. "What do you mean?"

"Oh, right, your phone. Here," she says, handing me her spare phone, which is about ten series newer than anything I've ever owned. "Check the group chat."

I open Body Swappers Anonymous. "Fifty-two messages!" I exclaim. I have a quick scroll through.

> **Ms. Callus:** Had a riveting lesson on algebraic equations. Ms. Daisy is a triumph.

> **Ms. Callus:** I'm perusing your past written work. We must talk about punctuation.

> **Ms. Callus:** Had to take over an English literature lesson on Keats where there were many, many errors.

> **Ms. Callus:** Remind me to sack Mr. Keen.

"Side note," Dana says, "you have detention all week."

"What? How?"

"Because *you've* been caught using your phone by five separate teachers. I had no idea people could get so addicted to using smartphones. Oh, I almost forgot—I have a surprise for you."

I groan. "No thanks, I'm all full up on surprises."

"This is the good kind. Come on, let's go to the bathroom."

Half an hour later I'm standing in front of the mirror smiling to myself. Dana was right: this is a good surprise. The dirty mouse-gray helmet hair is gone and my snap-on Lego person hair is now a brilliant shade of acid lime. I look like a K-pop star—or, at least, a K-pop star's hip grandmother.

Dana douses my newly dyed hair with spray and stands back to admire the result. "Welcome to the luminous yellow era!" she announces.

I tilt my head thoughtfully. "It's more a luminous green, don't you think?"

"Whatever it is, you're working it. I love the radium influence."

We spend the rest of the afternoon snacking, playing music, and dancing. Despite my old knees, I nail the "Hot Feet" dance, and the jerky slowness of my movements does add a certain charm. Of course, I don't feel fully like myself, because, well, I'm not, but with my new yellowy-green hair I feel cooler.

When we check around half past five, there are over 142,000 online entries to the "Hot Feet" challenge, some great, some good, some average, and some plain old wrong.

"Yawn fest," Dana says as she skips through the top trending clips.

"That one was great," I argue. "The dancing was seamless."

"I disagree. It was lacking a little je ne sais quoi."

"Je ne sais what?"

Dana looks at me. "You should enter, Skylar."

"Not this again." I turn away.

"It's boring watching perfection. When you dance, it's like watching the force of gravity compressing atoms in interstellar gas until a fusion reaction begins."

She's lost me. "Huh?"

"Yeah, in short, it's like watching a star being born."

I feel my cheeks grow warm. That's quite a compliment, and while I wish it was true, I don't think I'm *that* good. Sure, I practice a lot, I love it and I have what Mom calls "passion." But I don't know if passion is enough.

Dana sighs. "You have twenty-five minutes left to grab this amazing life-changing opportunity to win AZ8 tickets."

"My legs hurt," I mutter.

"Excuses, excuses," she sings. "You're always like this. Remember when you chickened out of dancing at the sixth-grade talent competition?"

"I had a tummy ache."

"Or that time in dance class when Ms. Ribchester asked who could do the splits and you didn't put your hand up?"

"I had the wrong pants on."

It's true, I did. But also I was scared. Dana doesn't get it. Her smartness is set in stone; she has the trophies and test scores to prove it. But my dancing is something I do in private. I don't know if I'm really good at it or not.

"I get scared, OK?"

"Get over it," she says sternly. "I can't believe a whole literal Woojin is asking you to dance and you're making up some feeble excuse."

"Feeble? I'm trapped in the body of a seventy-one-year-old."

She shrugs. "OK, so it's a passable excuse, but have you asked yourself this?"

"What?"

Dana takes my hands, looks into my eyes and I know exactly what's coming.

"What would Woojin do?"

What *would* Woojin do? Woojin, who left home at twelve to audition to be in AZ8. Woojin, who practices dance routines thirteen hours a day, six days a week. Woojin, who finished a live show with a burst appendix (though that's debated by some in the fandom). Still, the point stands.

I fold my cardigan-clad arms. "No. I am not entering. Especially like this."

"Why not? Think of how much you'll stand out. Like a blue morpho butterfly."

"AZ8 doesn't want old ladies in the Glows."

"That's ridiculous!" Dana laughs. "They make music for everyone—that was literally the name of their last album: *Music for Everyone*."

She's right. For a moment I forgot that inclusivity, along with great merchandise, is what makes the Glows the best fandom in the world. However . . .

"Their first album was called *Be Yourself and Yourself Only*, which I'm not being if I dance as Ms. Callus."

Dana mulls this over. "Fair enough, you've got me there," she concedes.

Ha! I love it when I outthink her.

"Still, I'm going to make an account in Ms. Callus's name, just in case you change your mind in the next twenty minutes."

"I won't," I say as I put on "Hot Feet" and grab another fruit chew to cheer myself up, because there's nothing like an unrestricted intake of glucose-based snacks and loud music to make you forget the pain of feeling like you're not good enough. "Oh, I love this song so much; it's impossible to hear it and not dance."

"Here, let me film you," Dana says.

"Hot feet, don't stop," I sing as I mimic Woojin's moves from the video; a high kick, a quick spin, a splash of vogueing. *"Hot feet, do the bop."* I mirror his cha-cha-cha, dab, and Gangnam before dropping into the splits.

"Woo-hoo," Dana screams. "Go, Skylar!"

"Hot feet, go whippety-whop."

Now I really go for it. I pop, lock, hop, and swagger, and it doesn't matter that my hip circles aren't huge, or my spins aren't super graceful, or my upper arms jiggle like jelly. When I get lost in the music like this, nothing matters, because I feel so completely myself.

Dana stops recording, looks at me, and says, "Whoa."

"What?"

"You're really good at this. It's so weird you can't see it for yourself." She holds the screen up and replays the clip. I guess it *does* look good, and there's something about being in another body that takes away the nervousness of other people watching.

"What time is it?" I ask as the clip ends.

"Almost six," Dana says. "Are you thinking of doing something impulsive?"

I take the phone from her hand and hit the upload button. "There," I say, and just like that, Ms. Callus has officially entered the "Hot Feet" challenge.

The next morning, the sound of AZ8's "Winter Days Are the Coldest Days" wakes me.

"Hello?" I croak into the phone Dana left me.

"Skylar, it's me."

"Dana?" I yawn. "Is it Friday yet?"

"No," she says in a weird, jittery voice. "It's only Wednesday, and you need to get to school as quickly as you can because I'm about to explode from a buildup of endorphins."

"What's happened?" I sit up gingerly, my back aching from last night's dance marathon. "Why do you sound so strange? Did your parents finally agree to go carbon-neutral?"

"Let's just say your impulsiveness paid off."

"You think I'm impulsive?"

"Just get here quickly," she orders.

I speedily grab an outfit, another pastel-colored twinset, some matching pinchy heels, and . . . ooh, what's this? I find a box of big hairclips with feathers, flowers, and fake birds—the kind posh ladies wear when they go to watch horse racing. I stick a couple of them around my radium-colored helmet hair, making it look like the most beautiful bird's nest.

When I arrive at school—after getting the taxi driver to take a quick detour via the drive-through where I pick up breakfast—Dana is standing by Mr. Idle's desk outside Ms. Callus's office and hopping from foot to foot.

"You're finally here then," Mr. Idle grumbles as he turns down the bubbles on the foot spa under his desk. "And you're wearing fascinators?"

"Fascinators?" I say as I stroke the birds in my hair. "Yes, they are quite fascinating, aren't they? And do you like my makeup?"

He snorts. "If you want my opinions on your appearance, you'll need to add it to my job description and adjust my pay accordingly. Now, this young lady claims she has an appointment with you."

"Yes, yes, I do, I do," Dana gabbles.

Mr. Idle squints at me. "Ms. Callus, could this *appointment* wait? Your schedule is packed today and I'm far too busy to keep telling people, 'Please wait here till the principal can see you.'"

"Can't we just cancel all the other stuff?" I ask. "Yes, let's tell everyone else who needs to see me that I have an infectious disease. Hand, foot, and mouth disease. That should do it."

"In that case . . ." he starts, but I don't hear the end as Dana pushes me into my office and slams the door shut.

I roll up my sleeves to check for the lying rash. Nope. It's definitely not a thing anymore.

Dana's face is red and flushed, like it gets when the UK Space Agency makes an announcement. We sit on the desk next to each other and she places her phone in the middle.

"Look!" she says excitedly.

Overnight, my entry has been trending worldwide, alongside other most viewed videos such as "Toilet Cleaning Hacks to Change Your Life" and "Squirrel Does Yoga in the Snow."

No way! Even in the few moments it takes me to eat a hash brown with maple syrup, the numbers of watched, liked, and shared zoom up. My entry has now been viewed tens of thousands of times.

"What. The. Heck. Dana, is this real?"

"Look at these numbers," she shouts.

"I am. I am."

"You know what this means?"

"That I'm more popular than a squirrel doing a headstand?"

"No. It means you're in the top fifty. It means you have a pair of tickets. It means you're a winner. A winner I tell you. A WINNER!"

"Shh." I put my hand over her mouth until she calms down.

"Sorry," she whispers. "I can't believe we're going to see AZ8 this Saturday. *See* them . . . in real life, with our eyeballs, our actual retinas, in real life and . . . and . . ."

"Whoa," I say, "this is incredible. I'm truly overwhelmed right now."

"Me too. I can't believe we're going to see AZ8. Do you think I'll faint?"

I grin. "Yes, I think you will definitely faint."

We both stand up, hold hands, and spin around in a circle squealing "EEEEEEE!" before sitting back down to read the comments under my video.

I wish my principal was this cool.
Daniel, 13, Scotland

This is amazinggggly bombastic.
Americans vote for Ms. Callus.
Adam, 22, USA

This teacher is head of the litty committee.
Ayman, 16, Kenya

Teachers should be teaching, not dancing. This is why the country's going to the dogs!
Sally, 42, Britain

"Jeez, Sally," I mutter, "it's just a bit of fun."

There are also a ton of comments in other languages, exactly like under a real AZ8 video. French. German. Hindi. Russian. Malay. Afrikaans. And, of course, Korean.

"Where are the tickets?" I ask.

"AZ8's management company will have sent them to you."

"To me Skylar, or to me Ms. Callus?"

Dana rolls her eyes. "To Ms. Callus, obviously. I set up the account in her name as you were entering as her."

"Cool. Do you think we should make banners? I might make one that says *Woojin for Prime Minister.*"

Suddenly the color drains from Dana's face. "No!" she cries.

"I was kidding," I say. "You take the political process way too seriously."

"No," she says again, pulling her own hair. "The tickets. Do you have access to Ms. Callus's emails?"

I think this over. "No, I'm in her body, not her head. Mr. Idle signed me in to the computer before. But I don't have access to her emails. Oh, right. I see the problem."

"We need to get her email password, Skylar."

Just then, Ms. Callus bursts into the office. And yes, it is still super weird seeing her as me. She shoos us off her desk, flops into the big green chair, and lets out a huge lion yawn.

"Tired of being eleven?" I ask slyly.

"Ha!" she replies. "As if sleeping for twelve hours a day and not having to work is tiring."

For some unknown reason, Ms. Callus has chosen to decorate my hair with pink ribbons, the kind Mom stitches onto her Princess Pretty collection of pillows. She's also frowning quite a lot. I'm sure I don't do that with *my* face. She switches on her computer and rustles around some papers on the desk before looking up at me and doing a double take.

"What have you done to my hair?"

I pat it smugly. "I've updated you. Given you that K-pop swag."

"I look like a tennis ball." She frowns even more.

Dana pokes me in my side and whispers, "Password."

"What's that?" Ms. Callus snaps.

We both shake our heads.

"Why are all sixth graders so immature?" she moans.

"Um, because we're eleven and twelve," I say. "So you *are* finding it hard?" This is a relief to hear, because the last thing I need is Ms. Callus enjoying my life too much.

"No, it's not hard at all. It's an absolute piece of cake. So much rest, so much freedom, so much collagen," she says as she strokes her non-wrinkly hands.

I hate it when grown-ups lie.

"Do you know what day it is today?" I ask Ms. Callus as I lean over the desk. "Welsh Whelks Wednesday. I heard Chef is boiling the whelks to ensure extra chewiness."

Ms. Callus grits her teeth. "Yummy. There's nothing quite like the briny taste of British seafood."

"Of course, because I'm a grown-up, I get to choose what I want to eat. I'll probably order myself some chicken and chips to be delivered. Because that's how easy *my* life is."

Ms. Callus snarls at me, then turns her attention back to the computer. Again Dana pokes me. Inconspicuously, I start to shuffle around the desk. "I bet you need to log in to your very secret email account and catch up on all your work emails, don't you, Ms. Callus?"

"Actually, I need to see the news. Your parents have no interest in current affairs. I'm not sure how I'm going to keep up with world developments while—" She lets out a mighty howl. "Why am *I* a world development?"

Right there, on the news home page, is a giant image of Ms. Callus dancing. Though, of course, it's not really Ms. Callus—it's me.

"Oops," I mutter.

She reads the headline aloud. "'Ancient Principal Struts Her Hot Feet in Sensational Dance Victory!' What is this?" she demands.

"Um," I start, but really, what can I say?

"'K-pop sensations AZ8 have announced the winners of their "Hot Feet" online video contest,'" Ms. Callus reads, her voice getting louder and angrier with every word. "'The boy band challenged fans to upload videos of themselves doing the 'Hot Feet' dance with the best boogiers receiving tickets to their sold-out show at Wembley Stadium this Saturday. Winners include street dance crew the Veracious V's, prima ballerina Katya Alacosta, four-time world breakdancing champion Wex Blaster 3000, and seventy-one-year-old British principal Hyacinth Patricia Callus.' Explain yourselves!" she roars.

Her face is so red right now, redder than I ever thought it was possible for my face to get. It's actually chilling.

"We kind of needed to enter a competition," I mumble. "To win tickets to see AZ8. You see, we didn't get tickets because they sold out in minutes and cost a bajillion pounds each, and our parents collectively refused to part with that kind of cash."

"You put *my* reputation on the line so you could go and see those avocado-hating ragamuffins?"

"I never expected anyone to watch my video." Of course, deep down, I *hoped* they would . . . But the idea that so many thousands of people across the world have watched and hit the like button is *wild*. It makes me feel all tingly inside, like when I get a pack of AZ8 photocards and discover more than half of them are of Woojin.

The beautiful, catchy melody of "Hot Feet" begins as Ms. Callus plays my entry, and I can't deny there's a flicker of pride when I watch the way I take that spin, even in my old-lady body.

Ms. Callus doesn't seem proud, however. "You promised you wouldn't harm my position as a member of the educational elite, yet you've turned me into a boogieing internet virus. It is not befitting of a woman of my stature to be seen doing the cha-cha-cha."

"To be fair," Dana says, "you look great doing the cha-cha-cha."

Ms. Callus is now shaking; it's like she's about to explode my face. "This video could undermine my entire public image. It must be removed immediately."

Dana chuckles. "The internet is like the Wild West. Once something's out there, it's really hard to get it back."

"Nonsense!" Ms. Callus roars. "Get that young man who set up Facebook on the phone."

"I don't know what Facebook is," I reply.

"Figure it out right now or you're both expelled."

Dana throws herself across the desk. "Expelled? No. Please. I can't be expelled. If I'm expelled, I'll never be allowed to speak at the United Nations. I'll be thrown out of the Future World Changers group chat."

Poor Dana. I hate the way Ms. Callus is still throwing her weight around and being shouty even when she is me. It's like Monday morning all over again, and I'm sick of it.

"She can't expel us," I point out. "She's still a student."

"Oh yeah," Dana says as she stands back up and calms herself down.

For a very brief moment, something like fear crosses Ms. Callus's face.

"Ah," I say, "you don't like it, do you?"

"Like what?" she spits.

"Being powerless. It's a horrible feeling. This is how we feel *all* the time."

"I don't care how you feel," she sneers. "I'll only be in this debilitating state until Friday. When I return to my rightful self, I will rain many, many consequences down on you."

Dana looks like she's about to cry, and I try to stay brave. "I don't know what that means."

"It means I have no desire to return to a tattered reputation, so do one more thing to jeopardize my standing and you will not have a life worth returning to. You too, brainbox," she says, jabbing her finger at Dana. "Now, is my virus off the World Wide Web yet?"

Dana slides around on her phone, her hands shaking, then suddenly stops. Her mouth hangs open like it's ready to catch a big old fly.

"Dana, are you OK?" Alarmed, I grab her by the arm.

She looks at the phone again and drops to the floor like toast, jam side up.

"Dana? Dana? Can you hear me? Someone call an ambulance! Help!" I cradle her head and stroke her red hair away from her face. Her eyes flicker open and a tiny tear rolls down her cheek.

"Dana, are you dead?"

She grips my arms and squeaks, "Woojin has commented on your video."

8
CHIPS AND DIMPLES

Dana lies on a bed in the nurse's office as Nurse Nina slaps a wet tissue on her forehead.

"Ooh, cold," Dana squeals. "Did you dip that in liquid nitrogen? It's colder than the rocking, popping principal from London."

Nurse Nina tuts. "Why does she keep saying that?"

I shrug, because I can't exactly explain that "rocking, popping principal from London" were the exact words Woojin used in his comment on my video. My video! Woojin! Yes, Woojin actually likes *my* dancing. It's one thing when your mom or bestie tells you you've got skills, but totally another hearing it from an all-singing, all-dancing icon like Woojin.

"It's clearly some kind of hysteria," Ms. Callus says.

Nurse Nina looks down at Ms. Callus, prim in her school uniform and ribboned pigtails, and tuts again. "I wasn't asking for your opinion now, was I, young lady?"

Ms. Callus recoils. "Sorry."

Dana giggles as a flashlight is shined in her eyes then ears. "Oooh, shiny light."

Nurse Nina clicks off the flashlight and frowns. "Apart from a huge build-up of wax, it all looks fairly normal. Maybe it's something she ate."

"Actually," Ms. Callus says, "her symptoms seem more in line with shock. I've seen this sort of thing before. Back in the summer of 1982, I was volunteering with the St. John Ambulance at the Chelsea Flower Show when they brought out a seventeen-foot Mexican cactus and I—"

Luckily this cover-blowing story is cut short as the door to the nurse's office bursts open and a wounded kid wearing a PE uniform is dragged in, held up by two others.

"Nurse," they wail. "Ping-Pong injury. Nurse! Help us!"

"Ping-Pong?" Ms. Callus shouts. "My, my, that doesn't sound very educational at all."

She storms over to the wounded boy, who is holding his left eye and crying, "Will I ever see again?"

"Rocking, popping," Dana chuckles.

"You need to snap out of it," I mutter. "This week is weird enough without you going all goo-goo."

Her eyes roll to mine and she smiles. "Woojin knows who you are. He knows you're one of the real eight billion humans walking this earth. That's potentially two to three steps away from getting married. To him. At the concert, this Saturday, because you have tickets. Tickets. Rocking, popping tickets."

"Dana!"

She makes an effort to focus. "Why aren't you freaking out about this too?"

"Because I'm already freaking out about being seventy-one and a world-famous internet sensation. Plus, we don't have those rocking, popping tickets. Ms. Callus does."

"Ms. Callus has what?" a very wound-up Ms. Callus asks.

"Tickets for AZ8's concert this Saturday. That was the prize for the 'Hot Feet' dance video. They're in your name and email account."

A slow smirk, not unlike the super evil one in her portrait, crawls across her face. "Lucky me."

"You don't even like AZ8," I point out. Though I'm shaking, because I've known much stronger women than Ms. Callus go from completely uninterested in AZ8 to completely obsessed quicker than you can say *annyeonghaseyo*. "Please give us the tickets?"

Dana makes a sort of whimpering sound, then reaches out to touch Ms. Callus's hand. "Don't deny us this rocking, popping opportunity."

Ms. Callus laughs. "You children shamed me on the World Wide Web and now you expect me to reward you with concert tickets?"

"Coach Cathy is holding a Ping-Pong tournament," Nurse Nina says as she comes back over. "It's going to fill up in here in no time. Ms. Callus, I think you can leave this one with me."

"Very well," Ms. Callus says, standing up.

Nurse Nina gives her a funny look. "Young lady, I was talking to your principal."

Doh! "That's me." I stand up. "I'm the principal here, of course. Thank you for your hard work, Nurse."

I follow Ms. Callus out into the empty hallway to grovel like I've never groveled in my life. "Please, please, pretty please give us those tickets. We'll do anything."

"You and your little friend probably saw this week of body-swapping as an opportunity for hilarious high jinks and tall adventures, didn't you?"

"Um, I'm not sure if we—"

"What child hasn't fantasized about being an adult? About changing the world to suit their every passing wish and whim? Well, I regret to inform you, that's not the plot of this particular story."

"It's not?" I ask, confused.

"Certainly not. If you want those tickets, you need to stop drawing attention to yourself, and by that I, of course, mean drawing attention to *myself*."

"Huh?"

"No more abominable hairstyles, no more trying to be a *cool dude*, no more dancing, and no more going viral on the internet. Do I make myself clear?"

I sigh. Because even when Ms. Callus is not an adult, she still has adult power.

"I repeat, do I make myself clear?"

"Clearer than Haru's skin after a Hydrafacial."

Ms. Callus scrunches up her forehead. "What does that mean?"

I put my pinkie out. "It means you have yourself a deal."

We pinkie promise on it. While I'm gutted about the lack of high jinks and tall adventures, I know it's worth it because seeing AZ8 in concert is all I've ever wanted from life. That and I also now really want to swap back into my own body on Friday, though preferably not until after that math test.

I watch as Ms. Callus strides off, her back poker-straight in a way that makes me look taller. When I'm back in my own body, I really need to think about how to keep up that good posture.

"Oh, there you are," Mr. Idle says, interrupting my thoughts. "The phone is ringing off the hook upstairs. I'm a very busy person. You can't expect me to keep answering all the calls."

"Can't I? I thought that was your job."

"Yes, along with turning up on time, opening letters, and making coffee. What's next—having to write things down?"

I follow Mr. Idle back up to Ms. Callus's office, where he's right: the phone is ringing a lot. It's really quite annoying.

"Hello?" I answer in my most polite voice because I am now the very picture of perfect.

"Hi, is this Ms. Callus?"

"Yes, my name is Ms. Callus and I am a very respected member of the educational elite. How can I help?" Whoa, I am so professional right now. AZ8 tickets, here I come!

"Hey there, sweetie, it's so fantastic to finally chat."

"Great, uh, who's this?"

"It's your girl Darcy Delaney from K-popdontstop online, your one-stop shop for all K-pop news, reviews, and possible untruths."

"K-popdontstop? Oh my gosh, I loved that story you ran on Tae's favorite stripy T-shirts—it was such hard-hitting journalism."

"I know, we're brilliant," Darcy says. "Huge congrats on your viral success. It is so so *so* inspirational. Like, seriously, after I saw it, I totally thought about sending my grandparents a text message. So, what the five million readers of K-popdontstop want to know is who is the *real* Ms. Callus?"

"Um . . ." Is this a trick question? Journalists love secrets and I cannot give away the whole body-swapping secret. I think carefully before saying, very convincingly, "My name is Hyacinth something Callus."

Darcy laughs. "Yeah, I know. But like, really, *who* are you? What's your essence? Your story?"

"My story? You mean the alternative ending to *Noughts and Crosses* I wrote in English? Because, yeah, I did think it was pretty good."

"No, I meant *your* story," she says again.

My story?

I don't actually know anything about Ms. Callus,

other than the fact she likes floral prints, peanut butter, and students who can play Beethoven's Symphony no. 9 on the oboe unusually well.

"Um, well, let me see, I'm a principal. At a school. A school for children and—"

"No," Darcy says. "Your K-pop story."

My K-pop story? That's more like it. "Ah, you're talking about my origin story of how I became the world's biggest AZ8 fan." I get comfy in the chair and cast my mind back to the old days. "It all began when I was watching the ABCDGVP Awards. I'd never heard of K-pop before, and then these eight boys popped up on the screen and I knew I had to find out their names."

"I totes understand," Darcy says. "And what made you want to take part in the 'Hot Feet' challenge?"

"Well, I didn't get tickets to the AZ8 show because they were expensive and there's a bit of a cash flow issue at home."

"Aw, I'm so sorry to hear you're a poor person. Sucks to be you."

"I know, I know. Anyway, none of that mattered when Woojin announced the winners of the challenge would get tickets. I was unsure about entering at first—a bit shy, I guess. But the more I watched the clip, the more it felt like he was talking directly to me."

"You think Woojin was talking to you through your TV? Hold on, I need to write this down; our readers are going to love this."

"What?" I cry, alarmed. "No. Don't write that down. You'll make me sound crazy."

"No way, are you crazy too? As in, out of your mind in love with Woojin? How does that make you act? Does it make you angry? Does it make you shout at students? Does it make you want to track down where Woojin lives and camp outside his house and pelt him with cute teddy bears every time he comes to the window?"

"No. I didn't say any of that."

"Have you heard the rumor that AZ8 might allow the best dancers onstage with them this Saturday?"

My heart speeds up. "No way!"

"Yes way."

"I'm not exaggerating, but if that's true, I will literally practice every second between now and Saturday."

"You must really love AZ8, huh?" Darcy asks.

I sigh with happiness, imagining myself onstage with AZ8. "Dance and AZ8. The major loves of my life. Along with Tae's dimples and sour cream chips."

"Our readers are going to be so excited to read all about you."

"Your readers?" My stomach sinks. Is this an

interview? I'm not sure I should be doing press right now. What was it Ms. Callus said? Something about no high jinks. "Please don't put anything I've said online. I'm trying to keep my head down at the moment."

"Of course not," Darcy promises.

I breathe a sigh of relief, because I feel like I can trust Darcy.

"One more thing," she says, "can I ask your views on the new minister for education?"

"Who? What? Uh, no. Sorry. I need to go. There's a pupil with a pencil stuck up their nose. Goodbye now." I slam the phone down. I don't know if you've ever used a real telephone before and slammed down the handset, but it is a truly satisfying experience.

"Phew," I say. Glad I dodged that tricky question at the end there. There's no way I'm going to risk those AZ8 tickets by talking about politics. No way. From now until swap-back on Friday at 2:22 I'm going to sit my big old butt in this big green chair and be silent.

I complete two minutes of paper shuffling, which is boring and stressful, and then watch eight minutes of AZ8 on my phone, which is relaxing and awesome. One of the best things about AZ8 is that you get to see all sides of them. Sure, they're rich, famous, beautiful, gifted, and talented superbeings, but they're also real, regular people who love sitting around in joggers, playing games on their phones and farting while stretching.

After a while I give up on the work completely and settle down to watch a few classic episodes of *Go Go AZ8!* In one, Dig-D and Dig-C are rehearsing for a live performance. There are spins and lifts and ballet and jazz and tap. Whoa, they're so inspirational. I think about what Darcy said, about AZ8 inviting the best dancers onstage with them. That surely can't be true. Though Darcy *is* a journalist—why would she lie? I go to the K-popdontstop website and . . . oh yikes. Right there, on the home page, is Ms. Callus's big old face, and the headline:

> **Principal Believes AZ8's Woojin Is Communicating with Her via TV!**

Uh-oh. I read on.

> Ms. Callus, principal at Britain's highest-achieving school, has today claimed that AZ8 heartthrob Woojin talks to her through the TV. In an exclusive interview with K-popdontstop, Ms. Callus said Woojin was sending her secret messages through the media, including instructions on how to get to his house to deliver him a teddy bear.

> The formerly inspiring teacher broke down when discussing her financial problems and admitted she would not sleep or teach until she had perfected her backward shuffle. She also revealed she had stopped caring about running her school and instead now only cared about eating sour cream chips and admiring singing sensation Tae's dimples.

"She's twisted my words!" I shout.

The backs of my eyes prickle as I envision Ms. Callus hitting delete on the email with the AZ8 tickets.

"No," I cry. "Please no."

The article has been shared over five hundred times. What counts as going viral anyway?

9
BORE FEST

Call it a miracle—or perhaps it's because Ms. Callus simply doesn't understand the internet—but by dismissal time she hasn't found out her face is splashed all over K-popdontstop. She has, however, sent me some *very* detailed notes about a governors' meeting I'm expected to host this evening after school. While it sounds like a real bore fest, Dana explains that the governors make all the important decisions about how the school is run. She is extremely excited about its "world-changing opportunities" and has sent me a document titled *How to Stop Ruining the Future: A (Perfectly Workable) Plan for a Greener School (Version 6.2).*

Except I haven't read it, nor have I read Ms. Callus's notes, because everyone knows after-school events don't need preparation to be successful; they need snacks.

As I arrive back from the mini-market, I'm surprised to find all fifteen governors sitting around the conference table and a stressed-out Mr. Idle tapping his watch.

"Hi," I squeak. "Sorry I'm late. Anyone for a blueberry mini muffin?"

An elderly man with a wispy red mustache tuts at me. "Ms. Callus, we really must begin. We only have an hour."

"An hour?" I cry. "That's so long." I sit at the head of the table and shrug. "Welcome to my school, which I am in charge of. Yes. That's me and my job." The backs of my knees begin to sweat as everyone stares at me. "Let me check the agenda."

I look down at Ms. Callus's notes.

Item 1: Discuss the strategic development of pedagogy for achievement in the areas of . . .

Boring!

Ah, I have an idea. "Why don't we start by reminding everyone of our names? I'm Ms. Callus, and you are?"

"I'm Monica," the sweet-looking lady next to me says. "I'm Billy's mommy. I've been a governor here since my little baby began sixth grade."

A parent governor. Ugh. I'm so glad my parents are not interested in doing this.

"Billy's in tenth grade now." Her eyes mist over. "It feels like only yesterday I was holding him in my arms."

"All righty then," I say hastily. "Who's next?"

"I'm Margaret Loos, the local councillor."

"I know you," I say. "My friend Dana once made us protest outside your office about the lack of plastic recycling in the district. We dressed up as yogurt pots and shouted 'Plastic's not fantastic!' till we got sent home."

Councillor Loos pouts her tiny mouth and looks away.

"I'm Cyril, for those who don't know," says the next governor. "I started in education with Ms. Callus here, back in the olden days."

"Olden days," I mutter. "Try Stone Age."

"I'm Brenda," a lady at the far end of the table announces between mouthfuls of muffin, "and I came in off the street, as I heard you had snacks."

A stern-looking man in a Victorian cape slams the table, making the mini muffins bounce. "Why are we wasting time? I thought we were going to talk about discipline?"

"And we will," I say, "right after some chocolate raisins."

The scary man raises his voice. "I don't want

chocolate raisins; I want the reinstatement of the cane."

At this, half of the table claps while the other half gasps in horror; I'm definitely in the second camp here.

"No, no, no," a little woman in a purple dress says. "Children don't need discipline; they need understanding. The children are not the problem; the problem is the *problem*."

The whole table erupts again. OK, I can deal with this for another fifty minutes; all I have to do is keep quiet, and then I can chill out at Ms. Callus's place and watch endless AZ8 content. I might even do a music video marathon so I can brush up on some dance moves ahead of Saturday's concert. Ah, the concert. It's so close I can taste it, and it tastes as good as these Tangy Tastic fruit chews.

While the governors bicker, I get my phone out and check my messages.

> **Dana:** Have you brought up using eco-friendly glue yet?

> **Me:** Not yet. They are talking about behavior polices. Boring!

> **Dana:** What level boring?

> **Me:** Boring times googolplex.

> **Dana:** I love it when you refer to math in everyday life. #proud

> **Me:** How are you feeling, Dana?

> **Dana:** Like my nervous system had a party and my brain threw up on the carpet.

> **Ms. Callus:** Remember the deal, Skylar! Don't draw attention to yourself/myself.

Thankfully red-mustache man does most of the talking, and I get away with nodding and saying "Ah, yes!" a lot. Though it's hard to stay focused. I should never have stayed up so late last night. How are you supposed to know when it's time for bed without an adult telling you? I drift off a little, away into a world where I'm dancing onstage in front of zillions of adoring fans. Everyone is holding banners that say things like SKYLAR, BODY-ROLLING CHAMPION OF THE WORLD! and they're all chanting my name: "Skylar! Skylar! Skylar!"

I do a spin and shuffle, ball change and then *pow*, strike a pose. The crowd goes wild. "Skylar! Skylar! Sky—"

"Ms. Callus? Ms. Callus?"

Hang on. What?

"Ms. Callus?" someone shouts.

I flinch. "Yes, Ms. Callus, that's me; I'm her. What, what, what?"

The mustache wriggles. "What do you think we should do?"

"About what?" I ask.

"About what we were discussing?"

I peek over at Mr. Idle's notepad, only to find he hasn't been taking notes but is completing a *Star Wars* spot-the-difference.

"Yes?" I try.

Everyone gasps.

"Or . . . no? No."

More gasps. This is confusing.

"Actually, yes! Let's do it."

Mustache man claps. "Finally! I'm so happy you've agreed to this after so many decades of saying no."

Mr. Idle yawns. "Are we done? I need to get home. I'm deep conditioning my hair tonight."

My phone buzzes again.

> **Dana:** Inform them about turning the computers off at the wall. It can save 30 watts of energy a day. This is your chance to make the world a better place.

"Hold on," I exclaim. "I have something to say about the walls."

Suddenly there are too many eyes on me and I go blank. I check my messages again.

> **Dana:** Also, demand school starts buying zero plastic sticky tape. #SaveTheOtters

"The otters," I start, "they don't like sticky tape."

This time it's the governors who look blank.

"Otters?" Councillor Loos asks doubtfully.

"Yes. And the glue. And the . . ." I trail off. What is it now? I really wish I'd made time to read Dana's plan properly.

There's more buzzing from my phone.

> **Dana:** Don't forget to talk about the uniform recycling station, environmentally friendly cleaning products, and poop fertilizer.

How does she think and type so fast?

"I want to talk about poop recycling," I try gamely.

"Are you feeling OK, Ms. Callus?" the nice lady in purple asks. "You don't seem like . . . yourself?"

I laugh nervously. "Of course I'm myself. Who else would I be?" I didn't know it was possible for my eyebrows to sweat so much. My phone buzzes again, but this time I don't look. "Not poop recycling; I mean uniforms."

"What about them?" scary Victorian man asks.

"They're too brown. And ugly. Let's get rid of them."

"No uniforms?" Cyril looks shocked. "But you love the Saint Margaret's uniform. You designed it yourself."

"I did?"

"Yes. You even campaigned for under-sixteens to be required to wear it on the weekends."

"I've changed my mind. We can't expect to raise a generation of free thinkers if we're forcing them to wear mustard socks."

"I agree!" Monica says. "My Billy's a handsome little soldier in every color, not just brown."

It's a nice feeling to have a grown-up agreeing with me for once. Maybe I do have some good ideas after all.

"Also, can we talk about tomorrow's awards assembly? We only acknowledge the kids who overachieve, but what about celebrating the underdogs too? The kid who got suspended and bounced back, the kid who has never scored a goal during lunchtime football, the kid who manages to keep their head up, despite being banned from Bright and Brainy Breakfast Club, their access to morning Nutella and toast cut off forever." I take a moment to let this tragedy sink in. "Everyone cool with that?"

They nod their heads. They're actually listening to me. This must be what Haru feels like when he does his rap solo.

"I have more," I say. My head is suddenly like a glitter bomb, ideas firing everywhere! "Mr. Idle, you might want to turn to a clean page in your notepad because I have a gold mine of ideas right now. Are you ready? Well, I think it's time we put *aegyo* on the curriculum."

"*Aegyo*?" Cyril asks.

"Yes, *aegyo*, also known as the act of extreme cuteness." I stop to strike a pose and make a heart with my fingers. Super sweet. Brenda mirrors me, and while she does have a nice smile, chocolate raisins in the teeth is a bad look on anyone.

"Ooh, and I've been thinking of how to make these assemblies more hype."

Cyril looks a little worried. "Hype?"

"So, I'm thinking, Saint Margaret's gets its very own light stick. You know, like the ones you get at K-pop concerts. We could get it programmed so it flashes a different color for each group. Say, red for ninth grade, green for sports teams, pink for the *maknaes*."

"The *maknaes*?" Cyril scrunches up his little rabbit nose.

"Your Korean is worse than mine." I laugh. "It means the youngest, so in this case the sixth graders."

Again, more nodding. I can't believe it's this easy to change the course of education. Now, back to Dana's points. "I also wanted to say something about something . . . hang on, let me refer to my notes."

As I'm skimming through the lengthy document, a bell rings.

"Time's up," Mr. Idle says firmly.

I am aghast. "Already? But I have twenty-four points on water saving to discuss."

The governors are putting on their coats, collecting their papers—and is that a cane the stern-looking man is holding? Brenda stops to scoop up the last of the chocolate raisins and tip them into her pockets.

"Hold on," I try, but it's no use. They all leave, Billy's mom popping back to grab one last muffin.

It's such a shame I didn't get to talk about Dana's

plans to save the otters, though I know she'll appreciate no longer having to wear a scratchy brown uniform to school.

The phone rings. With a huge sigh Mr. Idle answers it. When he hangs up, I know there's a problem.

"Mr. Keen can't come to school tomorrow. His band just got booked to play a festival in Sweden."

"Mr. Keen has a band?"

"Yes, the MegaBytes. They're pretty good. If you like noisy stuff."

"So who's going to teach computing, then? How do we get one of those substitute people to come in? Do we flash a signal in the sky?"

Mr. Idle shakes his head. "I'm afraid we can't afford one. You just agreed to spend five thousand pounds on textbooks."

"Did I? What a waste of money."

"Without a substitute teacher, the school will have to use its reserve teacher."

"Cool," I say, "and who's that?"

Mr. Idle's face is stony. "You."

I gulp. "Me? I don't teach. I'm the principal."

"Fine, we'll get that tall boy in eighth grade to pretend to be an adult again. Though you'll have to run Mr. Keen's party after school tomorrow."

"Mr. Keen was having a party?"

"Ninth grade won the Code for Coolness competition and the prize was a party."

"Can't someone else do it?"

"Why would they?" And Mr. Idle actually smirks. "You're the rocking, popping principal after all."

"Yeah, rocking and popping," I agree, because, on reflection, how hard can it be?

My phone buzzes and I open up Body Swappers Anonymous to have a look.

> **Ms. Callus:** How did the governors' meeting go? Did you uphold my reputation by keeping your opinions deeply buried?

My stomach feels watery at this question and I'm not sure of the right way to answer.

> **Me:** I didn't do any dancing if that's what you're asking.

> **Dana:** Did you discuss the 73 points made in my Greener School plan?

What I feel at this question is worse than a watery stomach. There's no point in telling her by text, so I simply message back:

Me: Yes. They'll think about it.

Dana: Best bestie ever! #YoungPeopleSaveTheWorld

I feel awful. I wish I could tell Dana the truth, but she's just a child and her only worries are to do with irreversible climate change. She has no clue what it's like to run a school from the confines of a crinkly old body. Not to mention all the stress of the swap-back and getting those AZ8 tickets. I swear if my hair wasn't radioactive green, it would be gray. And now I have to hold a party. I find Mr. Keen's party planning document, which says:

Ninth-grade party to-do list
1. Book the hall.
2. Buy tropical juice.
3. Find jugs to put tropical juice in.
4. Get cash from school budget. Or cache. Lol!
5. Be cool.

He's only checked off number five. Great.

While it's more work for me, it could actually be fun. In fact, with me organizing, this party could—and should—go down in Saint Margaret's history.

I go online and order the essentials: cotton-candy machine, doughnut machine, smoke machine, and five hundred rolls of toilet paper. Then some extras: an unlimited fried chicken buffet, strobe lighting, a magician, and life-size cardboard cut-outs of all AZ8 members. I whack it on the school's magical credit card and book the legend that is DJ Jan van Jive, who promises to handle the music *and* cake.

"Right, that's done. What's next?" I look at the clock. Six p.m. "Ah yes, home time."

Except I have to go to Ms. Callus's cold, empty home, not my *actual* home, where, I wonder . . . is Dad limbering up for a run that will never happen? Is Nana telling one of her long, confusing stories from childhood? Is Jesse around and suggesting a game of Scrabble? Is Mom at the pool like she usually is on a Wednesday?

Me and Mom used to go to the Wednesday evening swim session every week, though since I started middle school, it feels like a weird thing to keep doing. I know it makes her sad, but she's got to accept I'm growing up. Maybe next Wednesday I'll go again, just one more time.

I send Ms. Callus a message.

> **Me:** I hope you're being nice to my family.

The reply comes instantly.

> **Ms. Callus:** Nicer than you, it seems.

Nicer than me! What does that mean? I'm always nice to my family. Aren't I?

> **Ms. Callus:** Earlier your mother commented on how delightful it was to sit and talk with me. She braided my hair and we talked about boys.

They talked about what now? My heart races. Me and Mom never talk about boys. Because the only boys I want to talk about are global superstars and Mom has explicitly said on more than one occasion: "I don't want to hear about those beautiful pink-haired geniuses anymore." Or something along those lines.

Also, Mom is braiding Ms. Callus's hair! I stopped Mom doing that ages ago because, even though it's the most relaxing thing in the world, I'm not a little kid anymore.

Then, a final message.

> **Ms. Callus:** Yes, all that chlorine in the swimming pool made my hair a mess.

The pool? They went swimming together!

What is this I feel? Jealousy? Regret? Fear around the idea of Ms. Callus in a bathing suit? I don't know, but right then, it hits me: I miss my family.

10
AND THE AWARD GOES TO . . .

Dana is back at school today and seems around 79 percent normal. I say 79 percent because as we sit on Ms. Callus's desk eating supermarket croissants, she occasionally does a weird little giggle and mumbles the words "rocking, popping." I could do without this right now, as our deadline to swap back is 2:22 tomorrow and I need her in top form.

Good thing I thought ahead and have brought additional nourishment.

"Here." I hand her a can. "Have one of these. They go surprisingly well with buttery, flaky pastry."

She looks suspiciously at the fluorescent pink can of E-2-Xtreme Energy. "I can't believe you're drinking this stuff. Don't you know how bad energy drinks are for you? They're full of stimulant compounds."

I shrug. "Dana, I don't know what a stimulant compound is, but it tastes great."

I take a large gulp of the sweet, fizzy stuff and instantly feel more alert, speedier, and generally like a more brilliant version of myself. I'm not allowed energy drinks at home, but I stayed up so late last night thinking about what to wear to the concert and how deep Tae's dimples will be in real life. Anyway, if I was a real adult I would down a large coffee, but I heard coffee makes you poop and I simply don't have that kind of spare time this morning.

"Cheers," I say.

"Yes, cheers to you for running through the main points from the Greener School plan with the governors yesterday."

The last time I saw Dana look this deliriously happy was when AZ8 launched a range of sustainable organic cotton T-shirts printed with soybean ink.

A horrible feeling of guilt rises in my stomach.

"I know this swap hasn't been easy on you, Skylar, but now you've had a hand in saving the future of our planet, I bet that makes it all worth it!"

"Hmm." Ugh. This is awful. I have to tell her the truth. "Dana, you need to know—"

Just then, Ms. Callus bursts in, and even though we're now days into the swap, I'm still shocked every time I see my body walking around with someone else inside it.

"Morning, Ms. Callus," Dana says brightly.

And just like that, the moment to confess has gone.

Ms. Callus looks me over, taking in my frankly amazing outfit, before shivering.

"I dressed up for the awards assembly," I tell her. "I found this lovely yellow silky blouse, plaid pants, and, based on your feedback, I've toned down the makeup."

Ms. Callus scowls. "I told you to stop drawing attention to *yourself* as *myself*."

"I'm not," I protest. "I'm trying to blend in, to be bland, to be a good Ms. Callus and get those tickets."

"And were you blending in when you were parading me all over the internet? Making my body jiggle around to a song with the lyrics *Feet have toes and toes like to shake*?"

Dana puts a hand on her heart and sighs. "Yujun's lyrics are so deep; they really make you think about life."

"Anyway," Ms. Callus says, "it's now Thursday. We're almost at the point of swapping back into our rightful physical beings. Little Miss Skylar, do you have anything to say about what you've learned from carrying the beautiful burden of principalship?"

"Huh?" I ask.

"What do you now understand about my life?" Ms. Callus snaps.

"Oh. Um. Well, I now understand that you don't just swing around in your office chair all day and that sometimes you do have papers to look at."

Ms. Callus narrows her eyes. "And?"

"And, uh . . . I understand that being old is very tiring. Truthfully, there's a reason I'm drinking energy drinks first thing in the morning, and it's because I'm tired. Ms. Callus, your life is tiring. There, I said it. I completely empathize."

Dana claps. "Well done, Skylar. Ms. Callus, is there anything you now understand that you didn't before?"

She huffs and folds her arms.

"Come on, Ms. Callus—there must be something?"

"I guess it is a little bit draining being told what to do."

Dana makes a winding motion with her fingers to encourage Ms. Callus to say more.

"And, yes, double math is a tad tedious."

"Much better," Dana says as she downs her energy drink. "Carry on like this and tomorrow's swap-back is going to be easier than trigonometry."

"Here." Ms. Callus hands me a piece of paper. "I've prepared a very carefully worded script for this morning in order not to rouse suspicion."

I read aloud the first line. "'Hello, and welcome to today's awards assembly: a chance for those of you who are dramatically underachieving to take a long, hard look at your life and try harder.'"

"Wow," Dana says as she reaches for another can, "that's problematic."

I hand the paper back. "I can't say this to other students."

"Why not?" Ms. Callus asks grimly.

"Because it's mean. It'll make those who don't get a prize feel bad about themselves."

"That's the point," Ms. Callus says. "Now, take the script."

"No, I won't."

Ms. Callus smirks. "Yes, you will. Because little sixth-grade girls who want to go and see little singing Korean boys dance around in glittery jackets this Saturday do as they are told." She pushes the paper back into my hand. "Now, I must go. Nana is picking me up in five minutes for my dentist appointment. I'll be back in school for lunch. Remember, do not deviate."

Then, with a swish of her pigtails, she leaves.

"What does *deviate* mean?" I ask Dana as I pop open another can of E-2-Xtreme Energy.

Dana crushes her now empty can against her forehead. "I think she means do what she tells you to. Like don't be your usual impulsive self."

"You think I'm impulsive?"

Dana mulls this over, then says, "A tiny bit."

It's five minutes until the assembly bell. We do some quick stretches, because it always helps to stretch out muscles pre-assembly.

"I might have another tiny drink before we go," I say.

"Go for it. This is already my third. This stuff is so nice." Dana reads the ingredients on the can. "I don't know what taurine and niacinamide are, but I know I love them."

"Me too!" I shout as I give her a high five.

We do a few quick star jumps. I manage forty-two before I fall over laughing but Dana keeps going.

"Fifty-one, fifty-two, fifty-three," she counts. "Man, I have no idea why we aren't allowed these drinks all the time. Look how bouncy they make us. I feel like I could do anything right now. Quick, give me an equation to solve."

"Um, what's the square root of fifty-nine?"

"That doesn't make sense." She laughs. "Let's jog."

We jog on the spot, seeing who can go the fastest.

"I'm a human bobsled!" I yell.

"Me too. We should enter the Olympics."

The bell rings and we finish off the last of our drinks. It's assembly time.

"I have an idea," I say. "A way to zhuzh up this prize-giving. Book tokens and protractors? Ugh, no one wants that stuff as a reward for working their tiny butts off in chemistry. Who needs a protractor these days anyway? This isn't eighteenth-century Italy."

"Tell me about it," Dana agrees. "Why don't they ever give something good, like a really high-quality poster of the periodic table?"

"What? No. I was thinking more along the lines of an online voucher."

"Oh yeah, course, me too."

I hit the return key to wake up Ms. Callus's computer, where earlier today Mr. Idle had logged me in again. Though sadly not in to her emails. "This school credit card is amazing; it never seems to run out of credit. I just keep spending and spending. Here—get that printer switched on. I've got a load of vouchers coming out."

I stand in the wings of the hall and watch as the entire student body of Saint Margaret's files in. Whoa, there are going to be a lot of eyes on me.

"Nervous?" Dana whispers.

"I'm not shy, but this is intense. There's, like, a thousand people out there. It's crazy how often Ms. Callus does this."

Dana makes a heart sign with her hands. "Hashtag empathy."

Yeah, I guess it is. Whoa, I really am becoming a better person, and I don't think Ms. Callus will mind that much that I've changed her script a teeny-tiny bit. Plus, she's at the dentist for the morning so will never know anyway. This assembly is going to be fire, like the ABCDGVP Awards, but with better prizes. I shoot a double-thumbs up at fellow Glow Anthony, who I roped in to helping, and AZ8's phenomenal bop "Brown Eyes Are Lovely and Looking Right at You" starts playing. When the bass drops, I close my eyes for a moment. My heart beats fast, my toes curl, and my mouth feels a little dry. This must be how Woojin feels before he runs out onstage to show the world why he's the greatest performer of all time. Oh my goodness, I'm basically Woojin!

This is it. Let's go! I run out onstage, mic in hand, and scream, "Saint Margaret's—make some noiiissse!" And they can't help it—they do. "Lemme hear you screeeam!"

Dana and Anthony run along the front row and encourage everyone to clap and join in.

"Do we have sixth grade in the house this morning?" I call. "Woo, big up the *maknaes*."

Everyone starts to stand and get hype.

"Good morning, party people, and welcome to our funky Thursday awards assembly! Can I get an ooh-ooh?"

The crowd hollers back, "OOH-OOH!"

"Ohh-wee-oh!"

"OHH-WEE-OH!"

Whoa, I am so full of energy right now.

"When I say Ms., you say Callus. Ms.!"

"CALLUS!"

"Ms.!"

"CALLUS!"

This is such fun. It's actually a shame Ms. Callus isn't here to witness me blowing up her assembly; she might even take some tips from me.

I sing, *"Who let the dogs out?"*

"WOOF! WOOF! WOOF! WOOF! WOOF!"

We do a few more rounds, and the crowd is truly in the palm of my hands, but then I get everyone to sit down, just like Woojin does when he's ready to sing a heartfelt ballad.

I begin my opening speech. "Now, I know life at Saint Margaret's can be hard, and it's not all fun and games. In fact, there is absolutely no fun and there are no games. Not even boring games no one really likes, such as Monopoly."

Several heads in the crowd nod in agreement.

"But I'm here to let you know that as long as I am principal, whether that be until the end of time or until tomorrow at 2:22, I'm here for you."

I carry on with my speech, and man, if I could sing, I would. Unfortunately, when I sing it sounds like something bad is happening to a kitten.

"Now, time for the most mediocre improvement award. Drumroll, please!"

The sound of every student stamping their feet is epic; it's like the roof is coming off.

"Aoife in seventh grade, come on up. Your homeroom teacher said you went from failing all subjects, to failing just three? That's incredible."

Aoife blushes as she comes up onstage and I put my arm around her. "We're so proud of you," I say. "Your special prize is an all-day pass to the Oxygen Zero Gravity Jumping Center."

Everyone cheers and little pink-faced Aoife clutches the voucher to her chest as she cries happy tears.

"Next up is the prize for the student who managed to remember their PE uniform not once, not twice, but *four* times this entire half-term. Give it up for Max in tenth grade. Come and get your prize: a chocolate-making workshop for two. Woo-hoo!"

Max runs through the crowd, slapping palms, and I notice he's not in uniform today but hey, he tried.

Dana leans close to me and murmurs in my ear, "You should do the real prizes next."

"These are the real prizes," I say off mic.

"What about the prizes for the actual achievers?" she asks.

But I don't have time to talk about this with her now. I step away from Dana to the front of the stage. "Now, for an award that is particularly close to my heart: the Woojin Accomplishment Achievement Attainment Award. This is to honor the student who has made all our mouths drop open with her remarkable dedication to learning the sport of parkour, including jumping off—though not quite landing safely—twenty-inch-high vaults. It's Nikki from sixth grade. Come on up!"

Anthony runs into the audience to help Nikki, who is on crutches.

"The prize is a ten-pound book token," I say, handing over the envelope before snatching it back. "Just kidding—it's not the eighties. You've won a weekend pass to Upchuck Theme Park."

Nikki drops awkwardly to her plastered knees and cries with happiness. The students go berserk.

Things continue this way for the rest of the awards. I notice a few of the teachers are sitting with their mouths hanging open, while others keep glancing down at their watches as if desperate to get back to class. What's their problem? They're always talking about celebrating hard work; well, this is exactly what I'm doing. When I look behind me, Dana is also not smiling. What's wrong with her?

The kids are still clapping, wild with excitement, when I finally say, "You've been amazing, Saint Margaret's! You shine bright; you sparkle like confetti. I've been Ms. Callus, the best principal of my generation, and I'm out."

I throw my arms high, soak up the applause, and then there's only one thing left to do—and that's a mic drop.

11
THE FALLOUT

"That was epic," I shout as we head back to *my* office. I'm so hyped I break out into a mini dance routine and start krumping all over the place. "Why can't all assemblies be like that?"

"Well, of course not all assemblies can be like that," Dana scoffs as she trails behind.

"'Course not," I say as I pop my back and jab my arms. "Because then I would have to be principal forever."

"No, I meant if all assemblies were like that, it would seriously cut into lesson time—and can you quit moving so much; you're giving me motion sickness."

I stop. What's her problem? Is she crashing after downing all those energy drinks?

Back in Ms. Callus's office, Dana collects her backpack and starts to leave.

"Where are you going?" I ask.

"I have biology in four minutes."

"You don't have to go. I can check you in." I hop into the big green chair by Ms. Callus's computer and tap, tap, tap, done. Dana Popa present. "While I'm here, I'll change all the bullies from present to absent. This is hilarious. Why haven't we done more stuff like this? Let's see how Rayan Khan's mom feels about him missing a week of school."

"I don't think you should be doing that," Dana says.

"It's fine. I'm in charge. I'm the prin—"

"Principal, I know; you've said. Lots of times. Though it doesn't mean you have to behave like this."

"Like what?"

Dana is always super excited and happy, or super outraged and angry, so when she's neither of these things it's kind of unsettling.

"What's wrong?" I ask. "Did you catch the custodians mixing the recycling again?"

"No. It's more that . . . well . . ." She twists her mouth. "I didn't realize you were going to change *all* the prizes. I know it's good to reward people who don't usually get prizes, but there are also *some people* who really need the hit of dopamine that only winning can give."

"Like who?"

"Like me."

"You! Dana, you get a prize for something every week. Your family has a storage unit for them."

"I was expecting to win the Saint Margaret's in the Community Award today. I spent over fifty hours playing dominoes with old people last term and, as much as I enjoy being a good, selfless citizen, the elderly have no regard for rules."

I can't believe she cares so much. It's just a prize. Why can't she see the bigger picture?

"I know what'll cheer you up. I'm going to show you something brilliant." I rummage in the desk drawers for the special posters I had Mr. Idle photocopy for me in exchange for letting him leave early today.

"Is it the energy-saving light bulbs I suggested?" Dana asks.

"Um, not exactly." I hold up a poster. "Check this out. I've changed the extracurricular clubs schedule. I know Ms. Callus said to keep my head down, but I doubt she'll notice this."

MONDAY
YouTube Lunch Hour
Watch new and classic

K-pop videos.

TUESDAY
After-School Dance Club
Come and shake your thang!

WEDNESDAY
Breakfast Rap Battle
Bring your skills to our cypher.

THURSDAY
K-pop Chic
Get advice on your own personal style and look. Explore hair colors.

FRIDAY
Chill Club
A free pass to skip lessons, lie back, and relax. Talk to others about how adults are trying to ruin your life (bring your own beanbag).

"Are you serious?" Dana explodes. "Where's Crack of Dawn STEM Club? Where's Midday Masters of Mathematics? Where's After-School Eco-Warriors?"

I lean back and put my feet on the desk. "We don't need those anymore."

"It's not about *need*, Skylar. Maybe some of us *want* them."

I snort. "Why would anyone want to inflate a balloon with dry ice before school when they could be dying their hair tangerine orange and breaking a sweat to some K-pop bangers?"

"You're going to ruin everything," Dana snaps.

"No, I'm trying to help, so that when I'm eleven again things will be better. I'm trying to cut down the amount of our youth we waste on being educated and stimulated so we have more time for our interests, such as AZ8."

Dana's cheeks are now as red as her hair. What *is* her problem?

"You've got to understand my POV, Dana. I'm thinking about everyone here, even those weirdos outside of the fandom with niche interests such as team sports and playing instruments. No one should have to worry about their time being sucked up by so many pointless educational clubs."

"Maybe I like those clubs, Skylar."

"You're always saying they take up too much time."

"Yeah, and they do. But I can't give myself more hours in the day. I've looked into it and the physics is impossible."

"I'm doing you a favor," I argue. "I'm doing *every* student here a favor."

"No, you're not." Dana leans over the desk and jabs her finger at me. "You're doing what *you* think will work for YOU. But it's not fair. It needs to work for everyone."

"Why are you being so annoying about this?"

Dana gasps. "Annoying?"

"Yes. You're supposed to be my best friend. You're supposed to support me when I do things like organize a breakfast rap battle or change the course of education forever."

Dana stomps a foot. "I've supported you nonstop. That's all I've done this week. Do you have any idea how behind I am on my genetics and evolution project?"

"And do you have any idea how much pressure I'm under trying to run a whole literal school? And keep Ms. Callus happy so she'll give us those tickets? No, of course you don't, because even though you're smart you're still just a kid. You don't understand anything."

Dana recoils and her bottom lip trembles.

Whoops. Did I take it too far? I'm not sure, because we've never argued like this before.

Maybe I need to backtrack, to apologize, to talk about things properly; but then Dana says, "You know what, Skylar? I'll be happy at 2:22 tomorrow when things are back to normal. I'll be happy to have Ms. Callus back in this office."

Ms. Callus? Over me? I can't believe she just said that!

"You should go to your precious lesson now." My voice wobbles. "I don't need you to help me run the school anymore. The same way, if Ms. Callus gives me those tickets, I don't need you to come to the concert with me either."

Dana flinches, then shouts back, "Fine!" She turns and marches out.

"Yeah, it is fine!" I bellow at the door as it slams behind her.

"My school is going to be the best," I tell myself, because there's no one else to tell. Because I no longer have a bestie.

When I calm down, I order myself a green pepper, pineapple, and pepperoni pizza and eat it alone in the office. So very, very alone.

At least I still have AZ8, I think as I go on YouTube.

I watch a *Go Go AZ8!* where Dig-C and Woojin have to wash dishes while blindfolded and jet-skiing. It's usually one of my favorite episodes; it's so funny seeing the two youngest members, who are also besties, make a mess of every challenge. I wish someone was here to laugh and joke with me. Instead, all I have is unconquerable power and online fame.

Ugh. I feel so flat this afternoon.

"I need to snap out of this," I say as I pull up my own "Hot Feet" video. It now has over half a million views and around twenty thousand likes. Knowing so many people have seen me dance and taken joy from it is crazy. It's like a dream come true. Yet I still feel down.

The office door flies open and Ms. Callus comes in without knocking. "Oh, how pleasing it is to see you sitting behind a desk, working diligently and looking morose. Reminds me of myself." She shoos me away from the computer and tuts. "Not this humiliating virus again. Has it not yet faded into internet obscurity?" She grabs a slice of pizza and picks off the pineapple chunks in disgust.

"No," I say, offended. "People love my dancing."

Ms. Callus cackles. "If you can call those jerky moves you do dancing ... It really is unbelievable what blows up online these days."

Two things strike me here. One, she's the type of weirdo who doesn't like pineapple on pizza; and two, how easily she uses the phrase "blows up." This whole time I've been thinking about how I can fit in as a principal and convince everyone I'm Ms. Callus, when really, I should have been thinking about how easily Ms. Callus can fit in as an effortlessly cool eleven-year-old and convince everyone she's me!

"How was the dentist?" I ask.

Ms. Callus points to a sticker of a smiley tooth on her blazer and says, "I was very brave." She hits play on the video and as she watches I swear there's a tiny smidgen of a smile. Mom always says I bring people joy when I dance. Is that what's happening here? Is Ms. Callus feeling joy? Or is Ms. Callus's joy coming from watching *herself* dance?

"My, my, that is a prompt spin," she says.

"It's Tae's trademark move. You like it?" I ask, a little too hopefully. Why do I care what Ms. Callus thinks about my dancing anyway?

"You must have worked hard on this, and if there's one thing I admire, it's hard work."

"Yes, I practiced for weeks before getting it right."

"That would explain the marks on the carpet in your bedroom. Mommy and I were talking about getting a rug to cover it. Especially as Kooks did a little piddle on it last night."

"Mommy?" I question. "Excuse me, I'm not a toddler. I don't call my mom *Mommy*. And Kooks?"

Ms. Callus smiles. "It was hilarious. You should

have seen the way Jesse swept in with a bucket and sponge. What a hero."

"Jesse was home?"

"Oh yeah, big bro and I spent hours playing Scrabble last night. Such a hoot."

Scrabble? With Jesse? A hoot! I see Jesse once a month. How is Ms. Callus getting all this time with him? It puts me right off my pizza.

A phone buzzes and Ms. Callus takes it out. I'd recognize that antique anywhere.

"You got my phone back. How did you do that? Mom and Dad banned it for a week."

"Yes, well, because I've been so spiffingly well-behaved, Mommy let me have it. Plus, as I'm no longer distracted by this AZA123 nonsense, she doesn't mind me being connected at all. Ooh." Ms. Callus smiles at the phone and then lets out a roaring great laugh.

"What?" I ask. "What's so funny?"

"Daddy sent me a deeply entertaining viral clip." She angles the phone away so I can't see it. "Meerkats do the funniest things."

"You're getting way too comfortable with my family. You're not supposed to be enjoying yourself this much."

"Neither are you."

"I'm not."

"Is that so? Strange, because since I got back from the dentist I keep hearing about your assembly, about how *entertaining* and *exhilarating* it was. Adjectives which have absolutely no business being in the same sentence as the word *assembly*."

"I don't know why they're saying that," I lie. "I stuck to the script and kept it as dry as possible. You really think I would risk those AZ8 tickets for the sake of a stupid assembly?" Even an assembly as dope as what I just pulled off.

Her phone buzzes again and she smiles.

I try to sneak a peek. "Is that Mom?"

"Stop pretending to care about your family."

"Of course I care about my family."

"Not as much as you care about those rainbow-haired singing waifs. You don't even *like* your family. No wonder they're so delighted by me. They keep commenting on how pleasant it is to spend quality time together."

"I'm eleven. I'm not supposed to like spending quality time with my family."

"*I* do."

"That's because *you're* weird."

"I love spending time with Mommy."

"Stop calling her Mommy. She's not your mommy."

"Nana loves me too. Oh, how she loves me."

"She's not your nana. You do realize that you're probably the same age as her?"

"Anyway." Ms. Callus's voice cracks a little. "It's only one more day."

We both stare at each other for a moment, and it's as clear as the fake reading glasses Haru wears when he wants to look intellectual that I have a problem.

I gasp. "You don't want to swap back, do you?"

Ms. Callus flicks a pigtail and sticks her nose in the air. "Don't be ridiculous, child. I can't wait to be back here, at the helm of this elite ship. I'm simply bursting to motivate, manage, or discipline someone. And oh how I am longing to be back in my own beautiful home to . . . to . . ."

"To eat a measly microwavable meal for one while looking over expulsion data?"

It's quick but I definitely notice Ms. Callus swipe a tear away before she answers.

"Yes. Exactly. Back to my life. It's been wonderful having these days of complete ease and joy and"—again she breaks away to wipe her eyes—"company. But my real life is calling."

"Do you even like being a principal?" I ask curiously.

Ms. Callus makes a strange whiny noise. "Like?

Like? You think life is a salad bar where you only choose the things you *like*?"

"Yeah. Except no, because I hate salad bars. I once saw someone sneeze all over a salad bar and it put me right off."

"Life is not about choosing to do what we like. Somebody's got to eat the boiled egg and diced beetroot, the roast vegetable couscous, the quinoa and sweet corn."

"Actually, I don't mind sweet corn."

"Little Miss Skylar, life isn't about choice; it's about doing what we *have* to do."

"That's not true. I've literally never heard that before."

"I do whatever my duty is. For example, this week my duty has been to endure being a child. Which I have done with dignity, grace, and boundless charm. And *if* tomorrow at 2:22 my duty reverts to being an adult, I will endure that with the same qualities."

"What do you mean *if*? There's no *if* about it. We're swapping back. All we need to do is stare awkwardly into each other's eyes at 2:22 and talk about empathy and this will all be over. I get back my body, my life, and my family, and you get to shout at people again."

"Of course," Ms. Callus says as she hops up from the

chair with youthful ease. "We will swap back and you will have your tickets."

The tickets. I *should* be elated, but instead I just feel icky because there's only one person on this entire planet I'd want to sit next to and burst my eardrums with at an AZ8 show . . . and that's Dana.

Ms. Callus taps at the desk nervously and looks away. Something's not right.

"You will be there?" I ask. "Tomorrow for the swap-back?"

She looks at the floor and bites her lip. "Yes."

I sigh with relief, but as she leans forward to collect her backpack, her sleeve rides up and I notice a smattering of big red blotches up her arm.

12
FUN SPONGE

It's almost six p.m. on Thursday and here I am, sitting alone in the office and feeling deeply stressed about the following:

1. Ms. Callus was outright lying and doesn't want to swap back.

2. Dana shouted at me, I shouted at her, and we are no longer besties.

3. AZ8 might dress as pilots to perform "Fly in the Sky with Me" at the concert on Saturday and I'm not excited to see it. Not without Dana anyway.

Mr. Idle buzzes. "The ninth graders are here."
And now . . .

4. I need to be the party master even though I feel more like a party pooper.

Though, really, a party might be a good distraction. There'll be good food, amazing music, and the chance to dance. Dance, yes, that's what I need. Whenever I'm feeling sad or worried or bored, I put on K-pop and dance until my body is so tired my brain forgets what it was thinking about in the first place. This is also my chance to recruit as many people as I can into AZ8's beautiful fandom.

I stand at the gates and watch as the first group of students arrives. It's all very civilized and classy.

A little pink car pulls up and Rayan Khan jumps out. "You can go now, Mom," he yells.

"Take care of my little snookums," Rayan's mom calls over to me. "Make sure he sits down for twenty minutes after eating."

"Mommmm," Rayan moans.

"Come on, honey-boo, if you dance with a stomach full of tacos, you'll be on the toilet all night."

I cover my mouth so he doesn't see me laugh. As his mom drives away, Rayan pulls off his very dapper bow tie and blazer to reveal a black T-shirt with a picture of a skull on it. He turns to his friends and shouts, "Let's tear the roof off this party!"

"What's that about the roof?" I ask as he barges past me without a word.

He's not the only student who changes up their look and attitude the very second they're through the gates. All around me, flats are swapped for high heels, glitter is sprinkled over shoulders, temporary tattoos are slapped on arms, tracksuits are donned, and shirts are untucked.

Did no one read my dress code? I clearly specified K-pop chic!

"What's this about?" I ask a group of girls setting up a gazebo near the gates.

"We're offering spray tans," one of them says. "One pound seventy-five per limb. Are you interested?"

As I'm considering this very reasonable offer, I catch sight of Ms. Callus still in full school uniform but wearing my dancing bunny ears hat.

"This is a ninth-grade party," I shout at her. "No *maknaes* allowed."

She pretends not to hear me and walks quickly toward the entrance.

"Hey, hey, stop!" Wheezing slightly, I catch up with her under the balloon arch.

"Little Miss Skylar, I didn't see you there."

"Yeah, right. Why are you here?" I ask.

"Maybe I'm interested in seeing how you handle the delicate act of upholding school standards while keeping a leash on excessive levels of student joy."

"So you *do* still care about your school?" I ask cleverly, because if she admits to caring that means she still wants to swap back.

Ms. Callus thinks it over for a few seconds, then says, "Ha! Actually, no, I don't care. I don't care at all." She limbos her way under the balloon arch laughing.

"Wait!" I call. But she's fast, and there are so many people I quickly lose sight of her. "Ms. Callus?" I shout, to a few strange glances. "Ms. Callus? MS. CALLUS?"

"Hang on," Hugo Barber says. "Aren't *you* Ms. Callus?"

My mouth drops open. "Ah, yes. Though sometimes I like to shout my name out in a public place, for fun. You should try it."

Behind Hugo I spot Ms. Callus boogieing—yes, boogieing—her way into the hall.

"Hey!" I call, my old-lady legs tiring as I try to catch up. "For the love of Garam's almost-too-perfectly-placed beauty mark, would you please slow down."

"Oh, what now?" She taps her foot impatiently. "Spit

it out; I don't wish to miss a second of this jamboree."

"I need you to promise you'll give me my body back tomorrow." I hold out my pinkie. "Ms. Callus?"

"Adulthood suits you, Skylar. The power, the access, the wisdom of decades, the—"

"No. I want to be me again. I don't like being an adult and I don't like being in charge. It's tiring, it's boring, and it leaves me no time to practice my dancing. Plus, I've lost my best friend."

Rudely, Ms. Callus isn't listening to my very heartfelt speech. "You did specify this party was only open to ninth graders who took part in the coding competition, didn't you?"

I think of the invitation I put on the school's social board inviting the entire student population . . . "I've messed up, haven't I?"

Ms. Callus tips her head back and laughs. "Oh, this is going to be a riot."

"I hope not," I say, but she's already off, wiggling her way onto the dance floor to the sound of DJ Jan van Jive pumping out a bunch of tunes that definitely weren't on my very carefully curated K-pop playlist.

At least the hall looks nice, filled with balloons and streamers and thousands of tiny flashing lights. The life-size cardboard cutouts of AZ8 look super stunning too, propped up behind the snack table. And, oh look, there's a nice comfy chair beside the juice jugs. I could really do with a sit-down—my heels are pinching and the music's already giving me a headache. I take a seat and, yes, this really is a good spot to tut at students trying to get second helpings of snacks.

"Young man," I say to a boy in a frog onesie, "I think you've had enough tropical fruit juice for one evening. Shoo-shoo, off you go." I slap my mouth to my hand. Did I really just say *shoo-shoo*? What's wrong with me?

But I can't think over the deafening music. It's terrible, full of dull beats, unfeeling melodies, and—"Goodness gracious! Was that a swear word?" Wait! What am I doing? Since when does bad language bother me?

I have a horrible feeling this is something to do with the swap. Perhaps as we get closer and closer to the end of it, I'm turning into an old lady for real. Will this be me forever, moaning about noise levels and needing a sit-down, the same way Ms. Callus is dropping slang and enjoying her life?

I have to stop this.

I have to do something to prove I'm still me. Right after I get the DJ to turn down this *infernal racket*.

As I make my way to the stage, some dim-witted

child skids through the middle of the hall on their knees and cries, "This is how I want to spend the rest of my life!" Another, who is wearing a rubber-chicken hat for no good reason at all, drops a yogurt on the floor and makes zero attempt to clean it up.

"Oh dear," I cry as I catch someone doing a very inappropriate dance move. "Cease wiggling your bottom right now or else I'll—" Stop it, I tell myself.

Someone else spills a chocolate milkshake down their front and I immediately launch over to hand them a wet wipe. Noooo! Where did I get wet wipes from? What's happening to me?

Just as I'm about to fully freak out, the beautiful opening notes of "Hot Feet" pump through the speakers.

"This one goes out to the K-pop principal," DJ Jan van Jive says into the mic. "Show us your AZ8 ticket–winning moves."

The spotlight hits me and everyone starts to gather around and clap. This is what I need. This is who I truly am. I'm not some grumpy old woman who hates fun; I'm an eleven-year-old who loves to dance.

"Come on, Ms. Callus," the DJ says. "Entertain us."

"Oh, stop it." I blush.

"Come on, Ms. Callus," a kid shouts. "Do that funny dance we like."

Funny dance?

"Yeah, do that thing with your knobbly knees," another calls as they mimic one of the moves from my viral video.

"I burst a blood vessel laughing at that," some ninth grader I don't recognize says. "I watched that clip a thousand times."

"Me too. Hilarious seeing your principal trying to dance."

Trying to dance?

The students start to giggle and jeer.

"Shake your old-lady butt," Rayan Khan shouts, and they all burst out laughing. At *me*! My face feels hot with embarrassment and my heart starts to beat really fast.

I push my way through the circle of students and out of the hall.

I feel so stupid. All this time I thought people watched my video because it was good, and now I find out people only watched it because they thought my dancing was . . . funny. Who else thinks this? Does Dana? Does my mom? Does *Woojin*? Oh no, this is terrible. Perhaps when Woojin said "rocking, popping principal from London" the translation was wrong and what he really meant was "rocking, hip-popping old lady with no dance skills who should sit down and stop embarrassing herself."

Aside from the echoes of cruel laughter, I can hear something else, a kind of chanting. What now? I follow the sound to the schoolyard, where a large group of students are marching and holding placards. The group stops by the benches and chants, "Save our clubs!" I squint my old eyes to read one of the signs: KLASSES NOT K-POP!

That makes no sense. Why would anyone choose education over Korean pop music?

"Save our clubs!" they shout. "Save our clubs!"

Leading this terribly timed demonstration is none other than . . .

"Dana?"

She takes a step toward me and shouts into a megaphone, "SAVE OUR CLUBS!"

I rub my ears. "Ouch, and also, what's going on here?"

She puts her megaphone down and answers, "A revolution!"

"Against me? Why, because I don't want to go to the concert with you anymore?"

Dana's lip wobbles. "No, this is about more than the concert. You were supposed to be my best friend, Skylar."

"I was . . . I still am. I still can be."

"Why haven't the recycling bins been delivered?"

"What's recycling got to do with friendship?"

"Everything!" she yells.

There's a huge crash from inside the school and someone shrieks, "Tie them up!"

What on earth? I need to get back in there.

"Skylar, I'm trying to talk to you," Dana says as she waves her placard. "The recycling bins were point one on my Greener School plan and I haven't seen them yet. And where's the bamboo toilet paper I suggested? The bamboo pencil holders? The bamboo cafeteria utensils? The bamboo—"

"That's a lot of bamboo, Dana."

"Also, when I asked the custodian about the plans to start using poop fertilizer, he had no clue what I was talking about."

Hmm, I do have a very vague recollection of Dana sending me a text about poop fertilizer. But I'm not sure what poop has to do with bamboo.

Dana's face goes red. "You didn't look at my plan, did you?"

I know I need to tell her the truth, but I'm too ashamed to speak right now. I drop my head and wish the ground would swallow me up and suck me down into the depths of Bad-Friend-Ville.

"Did you bring it up in the governors' meeting at all?

Did you even mention the otters?"

"Hmm, well, I know this is hard for you to understand because you're just a kid, but there was so much other exciting stuff to talk about, like—"

A huge boom erupts from somewhere. Oh dear. That'll be the fireworks.

Dana gasps. "You lied to me, Skylar?"

"I'm sorry." I put my hand out but she drops her placard to the ground between us.

"No, you're not. You're not sorry about anything. All you care about is yourself." She spins on her heel and runs off.

"Dana, wait! Please."

The rest of the demonstrators look at me like I'm no better than a snot-covered library book. And they're right. I did lie to Dana. I've messed everything up. I'm the lowest of the low. The worst bestie in the history of besties.

I walk away, back to the hall where . . . oh my gosh, things are now completely out of control. The music is at an eardrum-bursting level, the whole place is trashed, and the students are acting feral. Some are dancing on tables while others are conga-ing around chairs and falling over in big laughing heaps. Rayan Khan violently shakes a two-liter bottle of soda, opens it, and then proceeds to pour it all over himself. Another child, who I can't identify as they're wearing a Darth Vader outfit, shouts, "Who's up for roller-skating in the technology lab?"

"Absolutely no one!" I shout back.

This is so far from the utopia I had in my head.

I run through the crowd searching for Ms. Callus, who I find laughing and joking with a group of *my* friends and doing a dance routine I've never seen before. I grab her arm. "I need to talk to you."

"Oooh," Anthony says. "You're in trouble with the principal."

I let go as I realize teachers don't grab students. "You've got to help me bring this thing under control," I hiss. "How do I get them to calm down?"

Ms. Callus twirls her fingers in time with the music and bops her head. "What a great shindig. I haven't partied like this in . . . ooh, let me think . . . it must have been right before—"

"The Great Fire of London?" I try.

"Ha, ha," she trills. "Anyone for more tropical fruit juice?"

"Help me."

"No. It's not my problemo."

"*Problemo?*"

"That's what I said. I don't care anymore. You can have the AB88 tickets if you want. In fact, I'll send them to you right now." She takes out her phone and, *ping*, I hear my own phone alert me of an email. "There," Ms. Callus says. "Done. Now, I'm here to par-tay!" And with that she wiggles into the crowd, butt first.

Whoa. I have the tickets.

But what does that matter when everything else is going so very, very wrong?

Come on, think! What would Woojin do if his school was being torn to pieces by a bunch of party animals, and his best friend was rebelling against him, and he recently discovered he wasn't really an outstanding dancer but a mediocre dancer who people liked to watch because they found his knobbly knees amusing?

DJ Jan van Jive is now chucking large cream cakes into the crowd. Yes, cream cakes. Why she's doing this, I have no idea, but the students are loving it.

At the side of the stage one kid swings on the curtains, while over by the snack table another juggles with chicken drumsticks. And there in the middle of the hall stands Hugo Barber shouting "HUGO BARBER!" again and again.

Ms. Callus laughs as she does a little dance move,

and for a moment I'm hugely distracted by how when she moves in *my body* it looks so weird and stiff.

"Please," I beg her. "You need to help me stop this."

"Nope, nope, nopey-nope," she says, squeezing the pumps on the bunny hat to make the ears fly up with every *nope*.

"Why not?"

"Because this bash is awfully fun, and also I don't want to."

"Stop being so selfish."

"I'm a kid," she laughs. "I'm supposed to be selfish. I'm the main character here. This is all about *me*."

"No, *I'm* the main character. Aren't you worried what's going to happen when we swap back and you've got to sort out all this mess? Don't you think it's a good idea to start putting things back to normal now, before it gets more out of hand?"

"I'm not swapping back," she admits. "I want to stay eleven years old forever."

"You can't do that!" I shout. "You're the real Ms. Callus. This is your school, your life."

"I never had a life. All I had was work and strife. This is a second chance for me. Finally, a reward for all the years I've dedicated to selflessly educating generation after generation, with no thanks other than a box of chocolate seashells at Christmas. I don't even like chocolate seashells."

"What are you saying? Apart from the fact that you have absolutely no taste in candy."

"Your family is happy. I'm happy. All you did was moan about your life anyway. You finally have the power you wished for. It's all worked out spiffingly." She knocks back the rest of her tropical juice and turns away.

I run over to the stage, turn the music down, and grab the mic. "Party's over," I yell. "Did you hear me? I said PARTY'S OVER."

Unbelievably, no one nods in agreement that, yes, this party has gone a little too far and it really is time to be going home and winding down before bed with an AZ8 slow-jams playlist. No, instead they boo me.

"BOOOO!"

It's horrible. I've lost all authority. How can this have happened?

I look around for someone to step in and help me out. But there's no one. Dana hates me and has run off. Ms. Callus is too busy living her best life. And is that a cardboard cutout of Jungwon crowd-surfing? I'm only eleven; I'm not trained to deal with riots and protests and this many spilled liquids all by myself.

For the first time this week I feel so deeply out of my depth, and I wish more than anything that Mom and Dad would sweep in and tell me what to do. Because I really don't know. I don't.

"Please leave," I try again feebly. "Go home."

"BOOOO!"

Then, despite the fact I'm the one paying DJ Jan van Jive, she turns the music back up.

I feel the unwelcome sensation of the back of my eyes prickling and I swallow it down. There's no way I'm going to cry in front of all these students—I'll never live it down. I reach over and pull the plug on the decks. The music cuts out and everyone stops dancing.

"Cake her!" a voice from the crowd screams.

What?

Then another. "Cake her!"

Then more, until everyone in the hall is chanting the same terrifying thing.

"Cake her! Cake her! Cake her!"

I turn to DJ Jan van Jive in order to give her my best don't-you-dare face, but it's no good. She grins widely, showing a mouth full of gold teeth, grabs the last of the cream cakes, and . . . *SPLAT!* I'm covered. My eyes sting from the vanilla, my nostrils are full of cream, and my mouth is crammed with what I must admit is quite a light and airy sponge cake.

I wipe my face and look out into the crowd, which is now a sea of phone cameras and laughing faces.

"Go home!" I shout. "Party's over!"

13
A NOT-SO-FREAKY FRIDAY

The next morning, the news is filled with ... well, I'm sure you can guess.

> **Outstanding School Smashed to Pieces by Partying Hooligans**

> **Educational Protests Result in Five Arrests**

> **Parents Demand K-Popping Principal Be Stopped**

The news is so big and so bad that AZ8 posts a statement on their social channels distancing themselves from Saint Margaret's and the party.

> Dearest Glows,
>
> We know a lot of you were concerned about our welfare after yesterday's incident at Saint Margaret's Academy in Britain. Even though our music was played at the event and life-size limited-edition cardboard cutouts were displayed, we do not condone the outrageous party scenes that unfolded. We do, however, love you and hope you enjoy these photos of us drinking watermelon-flavored kombucha.
>
> Love forever,
> AZ8

I sink my head into my hands. I'm banished from the fandom, the only sanctuary I had left. This is going as badly as that time I was asked to show my work on the board during a math lesson.

The swap-back is supposed to be today, but there's no way that's going to happen with no Dana, no one to swap back with, and not a single rain cloud in the sky. Even worse, the concert is tomorrow and while I now have the tickets, I have no bestie to go and scream with.

"Oh dear," Mr. Idle observes as he comes through the office door. "It's not even eight o'clock and things are already going pear-shaped."

"Tell me about it," I mutter.

He puts a coffee on the desk. "OK then, I'll tell you about it. Coach Cathy is outraged about the state of the gym. Apparently, there are one hundred and fifty-two missing tennis balls, a fox asleep on the trampoline, and a cantaloupe wedged in a netball hoop."

"A cantaloupe?"

"And don't get me started on what the head of science has said about her garden, but it seems fried chicken and pond life do not mix. The tadpoles will never be the same again."

"Oh no." I take a tentative sip of the coffee and find it almost refreshing.

"That's not all," Mr. Idle continues. "You've gone viral again." He pulls up a video from last night of me being splatted with a giant cream cake. Humiliating.

The phone rings.

"That'll be the bank manager," Mr. Idle adds. "The finances are a disaster. Do you know someone ordered forty-six extra-large kebabs for the party yesterday? And what's this 'essential resource' you spent eighty-five pounds on this week?" He shoves a bank statement in my face.

"Hmm." I think back. "Maybe it was for a new printer cartridge . . . Oh no, I remember: it was for cookies."

"You spent eighty-five pounds on *cookies*?"

"Yeah, the teachers are out of control. Yesterday I watched Mr. Antwi fill a baguette with jam cookies."

The phone rings again. Mr. Idle ignores it. "This place will run out of money. We'll have to sack some teachers and switch off the lights. We might even have to cancel the holiday trip to Winter Wonderland, and I was really looking forward to seeing Santa this year."

"Ugh," I groan.

"And if you think I'm answering that phone for you, you can think again," Mr. Idle finishes as he storms out. "All this stress isn't good for my complexion."

I ignore the phone and message Ms. Callus.

> **Me:** What time are you coming to school today? We need to talk.

> **Ms. Callus:** I will not be attending school today. And I will not be talking to you.

> **Me:** We need to discuss swapping back.

> **Ms. Callus:** I told you already. I am declining the offer of my old body and life back. Please do not contact me again.

As I try to swallow the massive lump in my throat, Mr. Idle pops his head around the door. "I forgot to mention we're having an emergency inspection today."

"A *what*?"

"The school inspectors are here. That's who those people sitting around the conference table are. Good luck."

Slowly, I turn my head to look at the conference table, where—he's right—four very serious and very inspector-like people are taking notes so furiously that smoke flies from their pencil tips. Oh dear.

"Morning." I wave sheepishly. I guess they heard everything.

A gray-suited man stands up to shake my hand. "Good morning, Ms. Callus. I'm Rupert Rigg, lead inspector. Now, you've been here for a long time, so you know how this works. We'll watch some lessons, take some notes, stop for a baked potato and beans around midday, then watch more lessons, have a doughnut, take more notes and, around half past two, we'll meet again, have a cup of tea, and decide if we're going to close you down and end your career. Sound good?"

"Sounds great," I croak, ready to cry.

"Pretend we're not here." He claps, and the team of inspectors pull on plastic gloves and hazmat suits.

What on earth?!

They yank open the desk drawers, rummage through papers, and put my handbag in a large clear bag marked EVIDENCE.

"This all looks very serious," I mumble.

"No, no, it's fine." Inspector Rupert starts dusting my desk for fingerprints. "Though perhaps you could await your fate elsewhere?"

I take my increasingly delicious coffee and head out, passing Mr. Idle, who is, amazingly, tapping away furiously on his keyboard, almost like he's doing actual work.

"You can't leave me here with those people," he whispers. "They've given me this form to fill out and it's full of questions I don't know the answers to."

"Like what?"

"Like how many students we have, what subjects we teach, our full address including postal code. How am I expected to know all of this?"

Ignoring him, I take out my phone to message Ms. Callus again.

> **Me:** Inspectors are here to shut down YOUR school.

> **Ms. Callus:** I do not care.

> **Me:** They are here till 2:30. We swap back at 2:22 today.

> **Ms. Callus:** I've given you tickets to see the Blue 8 Rascals but I will not give you your body. Stop messaging me.

The hallways are filled with students roaming, slouching, popping gum, and using their outdoor voices. Worst of all, when they see me coming, they don't shrink in fear as they should, but instead point and snicker.

"Hey, Ms. Callus, want a cream cake?" one green-haired kid shouts, causing the gang of students around them to burst into peals of laughter.

"Shouldn't you all be in class?" I shout back, using my best principal voice.

"Class?" Kiwi hair sneers. "We come to school for fun, not learning. The new Saint Margaret's is a total joke."

Two days ago, it would have filled me with joy to hear this, but now . . . well, not so much. Because the new Saint Margaret's is what I'd call a little *too* much fun. It's quite frankly lawless! No wonder Ms. Callus doesn't want to swap back.

Students snicker at me, others sneer, some attempt to stick pieces of paper on my back that say KICK ME, which is unkind and a horrible misuse of school resources. I spot one student wearing a T-shirt that says HANDS OFF MY EDUCATION. I try to walk faster, but I'm not sure where to go because a principal without an office is like an AZ8 music video without a dance break.

Rayan Khan makes his way toward me, but I don't think I can handle another person being mean to me, so I duck into the nearest room and slam the door shut.

"Ah, safety," I sigh into the dark, "and also"—I sniff the air—"socks?"

I scroll to the messages from Dana and watch our "Hot Feet" video. Not the one that went viral, but the one of both of us we recorded on selfie mode. In the video we're spinning, singing, and fist-shaking, then Dana doubles over laughing as I try to do the Korean rapping parts. It's so cute and . . .

Gosh, I really miss Dana.

We never argue. I don't know who shouted first;

I just know I lied to her and put my own selfish interests above hers . . . and above the otters.

I take a deep breath and call her.

She answers on the second ring. "Hello? *Just a kid here, how can I help?*"

I swallow nervously. "Hi, Dana. How are you?"

"Well, my carefully curated brain cells are rotting after listening to Herr Schneider deliver an entire lesson on White Teeth in German, and the planet is on fire due to the unacceptable amount of carbon dioxide pumped out into the atmosphere from the party last night, but, apart from that, I'm perfectly jolly and well-adjusted."

"I'm sorry," I say. "I'm so sorry about everything. I messed up. You were right. I'm an awful principal and an even worse best friend."

"OK, I'm going to stop you right there. You *are* an awful principal, yes, but so is Ms. Callus. But you're not . . ." She pauses and sighs. "You're not an awful best friend, Skylar. You just got carried away."

"I hate that I lied to you. I hate that we argued. I hate that I forgot what was important."

"And I hate that I didn't try to understand what you were going through. Whoa, this is a lot of hate."

"I know. It's making my stomach hurt. I want to put things right. For you and the otters. I miss you, Dana."

"I miss you too, Skylar."

My heart feels as if it will burst. "I miss you like Dig-D misses wearing open-toed shoes in the winter."

"I miss you like Tae misses good-quality fermented cabbage when AZ8 is touring Europe."

"I miss you like Garam misses peach-scented hair gel when the fans buy all the stock. I miss you like . . . Oh, actually I've run out of ideas. I just really miss you, Dana. I want to be besties again, and I want you to come and see AZ8 with me tomorrow."

"Eeeee!" she squeals. "Of course! By the way, where are you? Why does it sound so muffled?"

I switch on the flashlight on my phone to look around the small room, which is filled with water bottles, blazers, burst footballs, odd socks, umbrellas, and a unicycle. "I'm in the lost-and-found closet."

"Ugh, the place PE uniforms go to die. OK, wait there—I'm two minutes and forty-two seconds away."

I count down until the door flies open and Dana climbs in and plonks herself across from me.

"Why are you in here?" she asks.

I think about it. "Because I'm lost. I'm lost in so many ways."

"That's profound," she replies.

"Ms. Callus doesn't want to swap back."

She gasps. "No way. That sneaky little old woman."

"I'm also old. And not just in an old body. I'm old in my head because I'm grouchy and tired and I'm checking the price of things and saying, 'Ooh, that's a bit on the expensive side!' and, worst of all, I've started to like the taste of coffee."

Dana gasps again.

"And the school inspectors are here, and based on how I've been doing so far, Saint Margaret's will be closed down by the end of the day. Though maybe they'll give me one of those pension things and I can move to the seaside and learn to knit." I start to cry. "I can't believe Ms. Callus is doing this. It's not fair. There's so much I've missed out on. Driving a car, going away on long weekends, paying an electricity bill, getting my nose pierced, reaching my full height, the whole working-every-day-for-fifty-years thing."

I cry so hard my snot bubbles. "I don't want to be a grown-up. I don't want to be in charge. I don't want to have to think about choosing a broadband provider."

Dana shivers. "Whoa, I got a chill when you said that. You need to get Ms. Callus to think the same thing. But in reverse."

"What do you mean?" I ask.

Dana mimics Ms. Callus's voice and says, "*I don't*

want to be a young person. I don't want to be amazingly cool. I want to be a million years old again. That's the key to you guys swapping back."

I shake my head. "She loves being young."

"Of course she does right now, because she's only seen the fun side of things. You need to show her the non-fun side of being eleven."

The non-fun side of being eleven? "I don't know how to do that," I confess. "Do you know how to do that?"

"'Course not," Dana says.

"But you know everything, and if you don't know, then I definitely don't."

"For the love of Galileo, you've got to stop this, Skylar."

"You want me to stop accusing you of knowing everything?"

"No, because obviously I *do* know most things. I meant how you think *you're* not capable or clever."

"I'm not."

"You've adulted for a whole week."

"Only because you and your genius brain helped me. When your brain wasn't around, I messed up."

"Puh-lease. My brain didn't help you live on your own, or convince a bunch of governors you were an adult, or make an entire generation of kids who never win anything feel special. Skylar, you're amazing, and the only thing holding you back is your confidence."

"You sound like a fridge magnet."

"And has a fridge magnet ever told you a lie?"

I think about it. No, except for the fridge magnet we have at home that says BLESS THIS MESS, because no one has ever looked at the state of our kitchen and blessed it.

Dana stands up.

"Where are you going?" I ask. "Aren't you going to come up with a mastermind plan on how to pass the inspection and get Ms. Callus to agree to swap back?"

"No," she says. "Because I believe you can sort this out yourself." She checks her watch. "It's only 9:29. You've got ages until 2:22. I'll help, but you've got to take charge."

"Wait—"

Too late. She's gone, leaving me in the closet with seventy-four misplaced articles from school uniforms and absolutely no idea what to do next.

14
OPERATION SAVE THE SCHOOL

I can sort this out myself. I can sort this out myself.

I stand outside the staff room door and say it silently one more time. *I can sort this out myself.*

While Dana's lost-and-found-closet speech wasn't exactly what I wanted to hear, it was probably what I *needed* to hear. Because she's right. I've done loads this week. Surely I can pass a school inspection, convince an old woman to swap back into her own body, and kick my coffee habit, all by 2:22 today.

I send Ms. Callus a message.

> **Me:** If I pass your school inspection will you swap back?

Ms. Callus: No.

Me: What about if I clean your office and fill your desk drawers with high-quality snack food?

Ms. Callus: Let me think about that . . .

Ms. Callus: I thought about it, and NO!

OK, so she's difficult. Maybe I should tackle the inspection first. I have the advantage of Saint Margaret's already being *outstanding* by adult standards. All I need to do is combine that with what *I* think is *outstanding* by students' standards, while simultaneously patching up any damage I've caused over the last few days.

When I step inside, the staff room is pure chaos. Teachers are arguing and shouting, chucking papers around, and slamming down mugs of tea super aggressively.

"Hello?" I call, yet no one listens. "Teachers?"

Nothing.

I grab Coach Cathy's whistle and stand on a chair. "Teachers, teachers! Please, can we have a meeting?"

"A meeting?" They all groan. "During tea break?"

Mr. Antwi pulls a pencil from behind his ear and snaps it in two. "Why didn't you warn us the inspectors were coming?"

"And on a *Friday*," Mr. Hardy shouts. "I had planned for the students to do a bit of busywork while I caught up on grading. Now I have to be inspiring."

Coach Cathy smacks a volleyball across the room. "I've been inspiring for weeks. It's almost the end of term—I'm tired."

Herr Schneider mutters something in German, which, judging by the redness of his ears, is also a complaint.

I nod. "Sorry, everyone," I say. "I know you're fed up. It's been a long week. But can you please do your normal thing of being good teachers for today so we can pass this inspection?"

"No!" they all shout.

"Why not?"

"Because the students are feral," Coach Cathy says. "This is what happens when you loosen the reins: they go wild. It's like a uniform-free day, every day. Complete carnage."

"OK, I know I've been a little slack on the students this week."

"You think?" she snaps back sarcastically.

If I can't get the teachers on my side, I've got no

chance. I look across the room, where the school motto hangs high on a banner:

> ACHIEVE OR HANG YOUR HEAD IN SHAME

I hate this motto. I hated it as a student and I hate it for the school I lead. I jump down from the chair, walk over, and rip the banner off the wall. I grab a marker and write something new on the noticeboard.

"WORK HARD AND SPARKLE LIKE CONFETTI," the teachers read as they gather closer.

"That's actually quite nice," Mr. Antwi says. "I like it."

I turn around to face them. "It's time for a new way of living and teaching. Teachers, assistants, custodians, cafeteria workers, you cool youth-worker people who everyone loves but no one really understands what your job is, this is it! This inspection could be our finest hour."

I pull up another chair to stand on, because is it just Saint Margaret's or are all teachers this tall?

"It's time to face our greatest fears. Fears of being judged, of being closed down, of someone stealing our Woojin heat-changing mug." At this, I throw a pointed look at Mr. Ben, whose cheeks go pink as he hides a mug-holding hand behind his back. "Look, I know it's

Friday and we're tired and everyone wants to go home and binge-watch AZ8 music videos while eating ramen, but we have a job to do."

Everyone is enraptured, I tell you, completely captivated. Mr. Idle even sheds a tear, though when I look closely, he's not taking notes on my awe-inspiring speech but watching *Up* on his tablet.

"Now, eight wise Korean men once said, 'When the going gets tough, the tough shake like a snake and slither to the dance floor.'"

Coach Cathy's eyes go wide. "I'm sorry, what?"

"Those are the lyrics to AZ8's phenomenal smash hit 'Never Give Up Your Prey.' What I'm trying to say is, we need to show these inspectors that our school deserves to stay open. Who's with me?"

Now, making a speech and getting a staff room of teachers on your side is one thing, but getting almost a thousand rebellious students to play along is quite another, so I do what teachers have done for generations. I bribe them. A game room in exchange for turning up to class, a uniform-free day next week in exchange for looking put together today, and a permanent ban on all non-essential assemblies if everyone starts acting less wild. I also, on advice from the student council, reinstate the original club schedule for those who want it, alongside the addition of a few new clubs such as Kick Back and Chill, and K-Pop Kool.

"This is life-changing," Dana says as we implement points from her Greener School plan, including putting unbleached bamboo toilet paper in every bathroom, ordering solar panels for the roof of the science building, and replacing the cafeteria's World Food menu with a locally produced and seasonal Love Food, Love Our Planet menu.

"Goodbye, food miles," Dana says triumphantly as she dumps the redundant menus in the new recycling bins. "I don't know why Ms. Callus didn't do this already."

I smile. "Maybe because she didn't have your big brain to assist her with ideas."

"Or your self-belief to make it happen," she fires back.

I peek in a few classrooms to find the students looking sharp in their uniforms, though some still with pink hair. And listening to teachers, though encouraged to share their opinions.

Best of all, on the HARD WORK CONQUERS ALL display in the hallway, as well as the usual photos of students who have won poetry competitions and Nobel Prizes, there are also pictures of those who've managed to get over fifty percent punctuality or who've passed their spelling tests after weeks of failing.

It's perfect.

Dana nods toward the display. "You were right about this. It's good to celebrate everyone."

I step forward to pin up a final photo, one of Dana playing dominoes alongside some old people. "Yes," I agree, "but it's also good to celebrate excellence. After all, I know you worked hard for it."

Dana flicks me a finger heart. "We make a good team."

I high-five her and catch sight of the time on her watch. "It's already after two. She's not going to come," I say glumly. "This is it: my life has been stolen."

Dana winces. "Don't give up. There's still time. She might be on her way. Why don't you message her one more time?"

> **Me:** Are you at school yet?

> **Ms. Callus:** I'm sorry, who is this? I don't have this number stored.

> **Me:** It's Skylar. I'm in the hall. You need to come ASAP.

> **Ms. Callus:** No. I am very busy at home eating a spaghetti-and-steak burrito.

At home? This is bad. I try to call her but there's no answer. I guess there's nothing left to do except stand here and watch as the clock ticks toward 2:20 and then 2:21 and then . . .

That's it.

It's over.

Dana looks down at her feet. "I'm sorry, Skylar."

"It's OK," I say, though it's really not OK. "I guess being young was fun while it lasted. And we still have those AZ8 tickets . . ."

The bell rings, signaling the final lesson of the day.

"I'd better go and find out if I still have a job here." My voice sounds broken. I *feel* broken.

Dana squeezes my hand briefly. "I know things haven't worked out like you wanted them to."

"Ha!" I laugh sarcastically, in a very adult way. "You can say that again."

"OK. I know things haven't worked out like you wanted them to. But I'm proud of you."

I nod, then slowly make my way up to Ms. Callus's office. *My* office now.

Mr. Idle is at his desk, frowning at some paperwork,

though as I get closer, I see that it's a sudoku.

"Are they ready for me?" I ask glumly.

He rolls his eyes. "How am I supposed to know that as well as everything else around here? Go in and check yourself."

Inside, Inspector Rupert is packing away the last of his surveillance equipment. He looks up as I enter. "Oh, Ms. Callus, is it that time already?"

"I'm afraid so, Rupert, I'm afraid so." I slump into the big green chair.

He chuckles. "You do look so very worried. I'm sorry if this experience has been stressful for you."

"You have no idea," I grumble.

"We don't usually do emergency inspections, but when we heard reports of the terrible things happening here, we had no choice."

"Terrible things? I don't know what you're alluding to."

The word *alluding* is very principally.

"We heard you were allowing students to wear their blazers inside out, that pets could be brought into class, that you had authorized an end-of-year trip to Australia for the entire school. There was even an internet rumor that you'd built a dessert shop on-site. It was very concerning."

"Did you find a dessert shop on-site? Because, if so, I'm going to need you to draw me a map. I could really do with a king-size brownie right now."

He puts a certificate on the desk. "It's a pass."

"Really?"

"Your records are flawless: years and years of perfection. We all have bad weeks. Just don't let it happen again."

I can't believe I saved the school. I'm a legend. "Thank you. Thank you so much," I gush, relieved.

He starts to head toward the door, then turns back. "This might be a bit unprofessional of me, but tell me, Ms. Callus, who is *your* bias?"

Now, this isn't your normal question from an adult. Usually when grown-ups find out you like a band, they ask something along the lines of "Which one do you have a crush on?" Cringe. Or they try to be cool and act like they know AZ8: "Oh yeah, those Japanese boys with the purple hair, I love their songs." Also cringe. But no, Inspector Rupert is asking about my bias, which can only mean one thing . . .

"Are you . . ." I start, unsure. "Are you a Glow?"

I swear he blushes. "Yes," he laughs. "I am. I've been a fan ever since I heard 'Let Me Inspect the Love in Your Soul.' It really spoke to me. I was so excited when I saw your video, because the world needs to know that AZ8 makes music for everyone and that their fans aren't all young, screaming girls."

"Of course." Though that description pretty much describes (a) me and (b) Dana. Or at least it did, I think sadly.

"So tell me, Ms. Callus, your bias?"

"Obviously Woojin. Though Tae is my bias wrecker because he looks so good in tartan and is great at taekwondo. Who's yours?"

Inspector Rupert checks behind him as if to ensure no one is there. He then takes off his jacket to reveal a Garam T-shirt, but it must be kid-size because it's really stretched, making Garam's face look all wide and weird.

"That's not all," he whispers, and rolls up his sleeve to reveal a huge tattoo of Garam.

My eyes bulge. "Oh wow. You're a real fan."

"Realer than Garam's perfectly placed beauty mark. I have all their music on digital, CD, vinyl, and collector's cassette tape."

"Oh yeah, cassette tape," I bluff. "I used to love sticking those together."

He raises his eyebrows in a look of confusion. "Have you got your umbrella ready for the concert tomorrow?"

"Why would I need an umbrella for a concert?"

"You haven't seen?"

"Seen what?"

He takes out his phone and holds it in front of me.

"You want me to watch the weather forecast?" I ask, puzzled.

Inspector Rupert hits play on the video and the smiley weather lady says, "The Meteorological Office is tonight warning AZ8 fans to prepare for freak thunderstorms tomorrow afternoon. Ninety thousand fans, known as Glows, are expected to make their way to London's legendary Wembley Stadium to see the South Korean megastars perform their sold-out show."

My breath catches. Thunder? Lightning? Wembley? Tomorrow?

Inspector Rupert stops the video and says, "It'll be a great chance for me to show off my limited-edition AZ8 rain boots."

"Yes," I croak as my stomach bubbles.

"Anyway, I think you're doing a great job, Ms. Callus. Sparkle like confetti," he adds as he flicks me a pair of finger hearts and backs out of the office.

This storm can't be a coincidence, which means there's still time for the swap, which means I'm not trapped as an old lady forever, which means I can still get my nose pierced one day. I jump up and down and break into a little fancy footwork around my desk.

"Yes!" I cry.

I'm reaching for my phone to tell Dana when Mr. Idle bursts in.

"I heard the news. A pass! Thank goodness all my long hours paid off. You're welcome, Ms. Callus. I know you couldn't have done it without me." He threads his arm through mine and starts ushering me out of the office. "Let's go to the staff room, then you can tell the others about my hard work and, dare I say it, my promotion!"

On the way, I notice that I've missed twenty-seven calls from Dana and one urgent "CALL ME!" text in the last ten minutes. I call her back and she answers right away.

"Dana, have you seen?"

"Yes, I've seen and I'm trying very hard not to pass out."

"Don't pass out. By the way, I passed the inspection."

"Hurray! Amazing! Whoa! You're awesome and blah, blah, blah! Now can we talk about how life-changing tomorrow is going to be? Because I would pretty much do anything to dance onstage with AZ8. Except commit a crime. Or hurt a small animal. Or use a plastic straw. Or—"

"Dance onstage with AZ8? What are you talking about?"

"What are *you* talking about?"

Just as it all gets really confusing, me and Mr. Idle reach the staff room, and as much as I want to keep chatting with Dana, there's nothing quite like the glare of every teacher in your school to make you put your phone away promptly. "I've gotta go, Dana; meet me outside the staff room in five minutes."

"I can't. My parents are taking me to the Future World Changers Conference straight after school."

"OK. Talk later." I slip the phone into my pocket and grin at the waiting teachers.

"Well?" Coach Cathy asks as she stress-eats her third fish curry of the day.

"We passed!" I squeal.

Everyone erupts into loud applause. They throw papers in the air, they jump on chairs, they whoop and holler, and I imagine this is the atmosphere in here each July when school lets out for the summer.

"You did it," Mr. Ben cries. "Ms. Callus, the greatest principal of her generation."

I wipe a tear from my cheek. "Thanks, guys. I really appreciate it. I'm so glad we're friends now and—"

No one is listening. Instead they're all grabbing

their coats and bags and making their way rapidly out of the door.

"Wait," I call, "where are you going?"

Mr. Antwi looks back briefly. "Home," he says simply.

"Oh. I thought we could hang out? Maybe we could have a celebratory bubble tea—"

Before I've finished my sentence the room is empty except for Mr. Idle, who's busy gathering up the abandoned coffee mugs and noisily stacking them in the sink.

"I can't believe it," I say.

Mr. Idle glances at me and tuts. "Me neither. My work here is endless."

"No, I can't believe that no one wanted to stay and celebrate. What about you? Do you want to hang out?"

"Not really, no."

"Oh. Well, at least you're honest." I sit down heavily on one of the tea-stained chairs and mumble, "What's a principal do on the weekend anyway?"

"Go home," Mr. Idle says, not unkindly. "Go home and see your family."

15
HOME

I'm so nervous my elbows are sweating. What if my parents suspect something? What if they're mean to me? What if I see them with Ms. Callus and realize it's true: they do like her more than me?

I think of Ms. Callus laughing on the waterslides with Mom, watching funny animal videos with Dad, or peeling twenty-seven cloves of garlic for one of Nana's experimental burrito recipes. It all makes me feel very icky inside.

Dad answers the door and I'm so happy to see his smiling face that I lunge forward. Dad usually gives the biggest, snuggliest hugs ever, but as I wrap my arms around him, he stays statue-stiff until I realize . . .

"Whoa!" I take a step back. "That was so inappropriate."

He looks confused, his eyebrows shooting high up on his face. "Ms. Callus?"

I clear my throat. "Yes. Hello. Sorry for cuddling you."

"It's, er . . . it's OK. I know Saint Margaret's is a friendly school. We had no idea you would be coming by."

I try to look concerned yet stern. "I'm here to talk to you about Skylar," I say. "She didn't come to school today."

"She was unwell. I know there was a math test scheduled, but she'll make it up on Monday."

I can't believe Dad let Ms. Callus miss a day of school, especially on a day with a test.

"Can I come in?" I ask.

Dad stares at me blankly. "Into this house? Right now?"

I nod. "Is that OK? I promise I won't hug you again."

"Oh, of course," he says in a strange posh voice. "Please, do come into our humble abode."

Humble abode?

I follow him into the living room, where Mom is sitting with her headphones on and shouting, "Don't you dare marry that sleazebag!"

"Honey?" Dad calls.

But she can't hear him over her audiobook and sewing machine. She giggles and mumbles to herself, "A beautiful sleazebag, mind you."

"HONEY?" Dad tries again as he pulls off the headphones.

"What are you—Oh, Ms. Callus!" Mom stands up from her sewing machine and curtseys. "What a nice surprise." She smooths her hair and starts chucking random piles of stuff behind the sofa.

I squeeze my arms into my sides to stop myself from giving her a hug. Though it's difficult, because Mom's hugs are soft and squishy and also smell better than Dad's.

"Honeybuns, Ms. Callus is here to speak about our lovely, darling daughter."

"Oh, sorry, I was listening to a . . . um, a podcast," Mom says.

"Which one?" I ask. I've only ever known Mom to listen to romantic audiobooks.

"Oh, er, it's called *Germinating a Genius: How to Make Your Kid Smart*. We love to listen to parenting podcasts, don't we, oh sweet husband of mine?" she says to Dad.

"Yes, we do indeedy. Because we're great parents."

"Here, please"—Mom fluffs the cushions on the armchair—"sit down."

Right then, Ms. Callus comes in. She's wearing . . . This is hard for me to say, but she's wearing a sailor suit.

"Sweet pea," Dad says. "Your principal is here."

I stifle an incredulous snort. Sweet pea? What's happened to the usual way he barks my name?

Ms. Callus sits across from me on the sofa and primly crosses her ankles. "Dearest principal," she snarls. "What a *lovely* surprise to see you here."

"Dearest student," I snarl right back. "What an equally *lovely* surprise to see you here, in this home, with this family, instead of at school, where you were supposed to be, especially earlier today at 2:22."

"I had a headache so I stayed home with Mommy and Daddy."

Dad squeezes Ms. Callus's shoulder. "Oh, what a wonderful child we have. Honey, let's make some tea for everyone."

"What are you doing here?" Ms. Callus whispers as my parents leave the room.

"It's my home," I say.

"It *was* your home. It's mine now. And they're my family."

"No way. They're mine and I'm prepared to fight for them."

"Fight? No, I'd really rather not resort to slapping and kicking. I am a young lady after all."

"Swap back," I whisper-shout.

"No. Can't you tell the time? It's over."

"It's not over until AZ8 sings 'Though the Curtains Have Closed We Are Still With You.' And that's not happening until tomorrow. At the concert. Where there's going to be a huge thunderstorm, which is bad news for Glows planning to wear Crocs but good news for people who need extreme weather conditions in order to be swapped back into their own bodies."

"I don't want to swap back," Ms. Callus snaps.

"Really. We'll see about that."

Kookie prowls in, and I'm scared she'll go nuts at me like those dogs the other day. She sniffs at my feet then bounces into my lap.

"Ooh, has my little Kookie missed me?" I nuzzle noses with her. How does she know it's me? It makes me feel all warm and fuzzy inside.

"You have a fan," Mom observes as she comes back into the living room, smiling as Kookie snuggles into my arm. "Strange, because she's not been herself recently. She used to follow Skylar from room to room, but all that's stopped this week, hasn't it, Sky?"

"Yes," Ms. Callus replies, more than a little angrily.

"How interesting," I say as I stroke Kookie's silky soft coat. "I wonder why that is. Actually, I too have some concerns about Skylar."

Mom puts on her concerned face and says, "Right. What kind of concerns are concerning you?"

"You may have heard about issues at school this week. An uprising of sorts. I'm afraid your daughter has been at the center of things. In fact, you might call her the ringleader. At first I put it all down to growing pains—you know, attitude, challenging her teachers, correcting their work. That sort of thing."

Mom gasps. "Challenging teachers?" she echoes weakly.

"Tut-tut," Dad says as he puts a tray down on the coffee table. "This is very concerning."

"Mr. Hardy was especially upset after Skylar interrupted a lesson on Shakespeare to announce it was, and I quote, 'an insult to English literature.'"

Now both of my parents gasp in horror.

"There was also a citizenship lesson where Skylar called the teacher 'vapid' and said the worksheet was, and again I quote, 'like something off the back of a cereal box, and not the good kind of cereal you get on the weekend, but the rubbish healthy kind.'"

"Skylar, no!" Mom cries.

Ms. Callus loses it and slams a hand down on her knees. "The worksheet had an incorrectly placed semicolon. What else was I supposed to do? Sit there and allow the whole class to be led astray by imperfect punctuation?"

I ignore her outburst. "So I'm afraid, Mr. and Mrs. Smith, I have no choice but to suspend Skylar for the rest of the term."

Cue another huge gasp. There really is a lot of it going on—no wonder my parents both look so light-headed.

"She'll be welcome back at school next term. Until then, I'll leave you with these."

I hand over a file, and Mom shivers as she reads the one word guaranteed to strike fear in the heart of any parent.

"Homeschooling?"

"Yes. Homeschooling. We simply cannot have this little revolutionary on school premises right now."

"Ms. Callus, please," Dad begs. "Are you sure there's not another way?"

"No," I say loftily, with a swish of my hand. "She must be homeschooled. All day. Every day. At home. With you."

Dad folds his arms and glares at Ms. Callus. "Looks like someone needs some tough love, and we know how to do that, because we've listened to the podcasts."

"Can I make some suggestions?" I ask sweetly.

"No," Ms. Callus retorts, before catching Mom's and Dad's angry glares.

"I'd start with banning books and Scrabble," I say. "As well as trips to the library and swimming."

"Swimming?" Dad says, puzzled.

"Yes, the swimming-pool changing rooms are where many gangs are formed. You might think your child is simply taking their time enjoying the feel of a hair dryer against their neck, but really they are plotting ways to disrupt education. I'd keep Skylar out of the kitchen too. Confine her to her room. Ground her. It worked for Rapunzel. Now, I wouldn't want her life to be all doom and gloom, so allow her limited but intense access to her interests. I'd say ninety minutes a night of K-pop should cover it."

Ms. Callus stomps her foot. "Oh, for good—"

I cut her off. "Might I suggest AZ8's Japanese mini-album *Teach Me How to Be Your Heart*. Just loop it and play at maximum volume."

Ms. Callus scowls. My work is done.

As I leave, Nana comes over and hands me a tub of what smells like sweet potato and chili burritos: my absolute favorite.

She pats my hand. "A little snack for you, Ms. Callus.

Being a principal must be hungry work."

How I've missed Nana's delicious cooking. Especially when I haven't had to assist in the cooking of it.

"Thank you, Nana," I say before I can catch myself. Whoops. "I mean . . ."

But Nana doesn't look at me strangely or ask why I called her that. She simply winks and returns to the kitchen.

I make my way back to Ms. Callus's house, kick off my heels, and put the lovely food Nana gave me in the microwave. As I watch the burritos rotating slowly, I ponder the wink Nana gave me. Could it be she sensed the real me, the same way Kookie did?

My phone rings.

"Finally!" I say to Dana. "I've been dying to speak to you. How long does a Future World Changers Conference go on for?"

"Not long enough," she says. "Anyway, I'm calling you to freak out about the—"

"Weather report? I know!"

"The weather?" Dana asks, sounding confused. "You know I don't watch the weather. It depresses me to have that daily reminder of how much the planet is overheating."

"So you don't know about the huge storm predicted to hit tomorrow afternoon, right over Wembley Stadium?"

Dana gasps. "No, I most certainly did not know about that."

"Do you know what this means?"

"That AZ8 will wear matching raincoats during 'Rain Can't Stop Me Dancing'?"

I squeal at the idea of AZ8 in coordinating rain gear. "Yes, but also . . . Dana, I think you were wrong about the lightning just being the inciting incident. I think we need it to swap back as well."

"That doesn't make sense," Dana argues.

The microwave pings and I remove my burritos. "None of this makes sense," I point out.

"So true, so true."

"So what were you calling me to freak out about?" I ask between mouthfuls of the best burrito I've ever tasted in my life. Gosh, I've missed home-cooked food.

Dana takes a breath. "Are you sitting, or preferably lying down?"

"Uh-huh," I say as I haul myself up on the kitchen counter.

"AZ8 launched another 'Hot Feet' online video challenge. This time they want 'Hotter Feet' videos. It's a way harder challenge: you can't just copy their dance; you need to make up your own. They said the best entries would get to perform onstage with them."

"Whaaaaat?" I shout.

"The only thing is, it's a flash challenge and they want entries in by six tonight."

I glance at Ms. Callus's kitchen clock. "Dana, that's in less than an hour."

"Yeah, and? It's a Friday night and you're seventy-one. Don't pretend you have other plans."

She's right. However, there's no way I'm dancing again. "No," I say firmly.

"Why not? Your last video was a huge global success."

"Only because it made people laugh." I can almost hear the laughter of those kids in the hall again. "People didn't watch it because they thought I was good; they watched it because it was funny seeing an old lady trying to dance to K-pop. And the worst part is, *I* thought I looked good in that video."

"You *did* look good, Skylar. Your moves were amazing."

"No." I slide off the counter and dump my dirty tub in the sink. "Let's leave getting onstage to the real dancers."

Real dancers? Ugh. This hurts. But I need to accept it.

"Besides, tomorrow is a big day for me. I still don't know if Ms. Callus will show up or not. Now, if you'll excuse me, there's a very nice program about flower arranging I need to watch."

"Skylar," Dana snaps. "You know there's no rule about *how* to be old?"

"What do you mean?"

"I mean, if you do get stuck as a seventy-one-year-old, you don't have to start bathing in Epsom salts and having your hips replaced. You can be a cool old lady. One who likes K-pop and dancing and radium green hair dye. The same way your nana is a cool old lady who likes reality TV, making Mexican food and shopping for knockoffs online."

Hmm. I've never thought about it this way. Though I can still hear the way those ninth-grade kids laughed at my dancing. It was horrible and humiliating.

"No," I repeat. "I'm still not dancing."

Dana sighs. "OK, bestie, I can't change your mind. I'm just happy we're going to the show together."

"Me too," I say. "Talk later."

We hang up and I go down to the basement and put the "Hot Feet" video on the TV, because even though it reminds me of everything terrible that's happened this week, it's still a banger. As soon as it starts, I can't help but tap my fingers to the beat, though I don't get up and dance. Oh no, because I'm past that. I'm a grown—

"Ooh, your toes are dancing; I love it when they're dancing."

I love this bit, and a little shuffling around in slippers never hurt anyone.

"Ooh, hot feet, don't stop moving."

I turn the volume up, because I am old after all and find it hard to hear things. Also, a song this good needs to be listened to very, very loudly to ensure full enjoyment.

"Ooh, hot feet, don't stop the grooving."

I throw in some flips and boogies, and it feels so awesome to move. When the song ends, the next video automatically begins. Before I can get to the remote control to stop it, AZ8 pops up on the screen, all eight of them, and they look so beautiful dressed in cowboy hats and fringed jackets that I can't bear to switch it off.

Garam begins to talk. "Are your feet burning up to dance onstage with AZ8? Do you think you have what it takes? We're looking for the coolest, most original new dances for our twelve-hour 'Hotter Feet' live challenge. It's time to show the world your skills and sparkle like confetti. Entry closes at six p.m. Friday. Let's go!"

There are already over fifteen thousand videos. Fewer than the original "Hot Feet" challenge, but I guess it's way harder to come up with your own "Hotter Feet" moves. I watch a few videos, which are OK, then scroll down to read the comments.

Where is the K-popping principal?
Ava, 11, Brunei

That teacher was a great dancer. Maybe she died.
Zoya, 16, Dubai

We need that old-person swag.
Florence, 58, Bermuda

Can Tae come to my birthday party?
Annabelle, 9, London

Then a comment from Garam himself:

Great entries so far, but we're looking for something different, fresh, and original. Is that you? Are you out there?

I think about how happy I made everyone at the awards assembly. All those students who had never before felt they were good at anything finally being rewarded. I did that. I think about Inspector Rupert saying the new Saint Margaret's was the greatest school he'd ever seen in his life, or something along those lines. And I think about Dana saying how much she believes in me and all those people online who *want* to see me dance again. But then, most importantly, I think about how much I enjoy dancing, how good it makes *me* feel, and how when I'm dancing it's like the truest me ever, whether I'm in my own body or not.

My ancient bones click as I stand up. I go over to the mirror and look at my crumpled face.

"What would Skylar do?" I murmur.

It's now 5:25 and I don't have time to practice anything, so I put on "Hot Feet" as loud as it'll go, hit record on my phone, and freestyle.

16
THE CHASE

The sound of "Winter Days Are the Coldest Days" shocks me awake. I jump up and pull an empty bag of tortilla chips from my hair.

"Hello? Hello?" I slur sleepily.

"Hello, is this Hyacinth Callus?" asks a lady.

"Who? Oh, yeah, that's me," I grumble. "Unfortunately."

"You have been selected for the 'Hotter Feet' live challenge."

I shake my head, because surely I'm still asleep and this is a dream.

"You need to arrive at Wembley Stadium by noon. The show starts at two o'clock promptly. Please bring identification to prove you are who you say you are."

"Whoa, whoa, whoa, slow down." My brain is having trouble keeping up.

"I-den-ti-fi-cation," the lady says very slowly. "That means something with your full name and image."

I shake my head again, more vigorously this time. "No, I don't understand the part about me being selected. I'm going to be allowed onstage? With AZ8? In real life?"

"Yes," she says plainly, as if being in the same space with AZ8 is an everyday occurrence and not something to scream, cry, or throw up over. She reels off more details which I find very hard to follow, then her last words are: "Latecomers will not be permitted."

She hangs up, leaving me to shout *"Arggghhh!"* which I think I do for seven minutes straight before calling Dana.

"Hi, you've reached the voicemail of Dana Popa. I'm unavailable to take your call right now as I'm litter-picking. If you want more information on litter-picking in your local area, please go to www—"

I hang up and text Ms. Callus.

> **Me:** Where is your passport or driver's license? I need it today. Life-or-death situation.

Ms. Callus: Can't help. Too busy nursing my broken ears after being subjected to hours of K-pop last night.

Me: Please help!

Ms. Callus: No.

I stomp around the house, opening and closing drawers as I search for identification, but can't even find a library card. Outside, the skies are darkening. I text Ms. Callus a picture of the thickening clouds followed by the message:

Me: Storm coming. You know what this means?

Ms. Callus: No barbecue for you tonight.

Me: It means time to swap back.

Ms. Callus: No.

Me: I'm going to school now.

Ms. Callus: Ha ha! School on a Saturday. I won't miss that at all.

Me: I will come by after with a new playlist for Mom and Dad. AZ8's Greatest Love Songs, the Taiwanese version.

Ms. Callus: 😒

Dana calls me back. "Sorry I missed your call. You won't believe the number of cigarette butts, chip bags, and takeout containers we found in the park this morning. What is wrong with the general public?"

"I entered the 'Hotter Feet' live challenge," I blurt.

"What? Whoa. You really are impulsive."

"And I've been selected to dance onstage with AZ8. Gosh, saying that out loud makes me lightheaded. We need to be at Wembley Stadium by noon."

Dana takes a deep breath.

"Don't pass out," I shout.

"But I . . . but I . . ."

"Dana! Do. Not. Pass. Out. Look, I need to get something from school first. Will you meet me there?"

"School on a Saturday? I thought you'd never ask."

I walk into the deserted school building and head straight to the main hall, where the portrait of the school's founder and original nightmare principal, Sir Charles Callus, stares down at me.

"I bet you were super mean," I mutter to the painting.

I pass under the other Callus portraits and stop beneath the snarling face of Ms. Callus. Except, now that I study it properly, I see she isn't actually snarling in the painting. Instead, she looks resigned. Like when you get asked to do something you really don't want to do, such as supervise your younger cousin as he plays with a suspicious brown object in the sandbox.

I grab a chair, reach up, and pull the portrait off the wall. As I stagger back down, I hear footsteps.

"Hello, superstar!" Dana calls as she skips in. She's wearing a T-shirt that says STEM STUDENTS FOR YUJUN.

"You're here! Are you excited?"

"Is the ocean floor mostly soil and hydrothermal vents?" She laughs almost deliriously before elaborating. "I am *so* excited, and as much as the jury's still out on whether humans can spontaneously combust or not, right now, I feel like I definitely could. What about you? Why aren't you excited?"

"I am excited. But I'm also nervous about all the unknowns. Like if Ms. Callus will show up. If the swap-back will work. If Haru will attempt a triple backflip while singing 'Your Love Flips Me Over.' There's so much I don't know."

"It's going to be OK." Dana pats me on the shoulder. "I'm glad you asked me to come with you today."

"Of course I asked you. You're my best friend. The yin to my yang, the Dig-D to my Dig-C, the noodles to my chicken soup." I pause. "Though I am seventy-one and you're eleven."

She frowns. "So?"

"So, if Ms. Callus doesn't turn up today to swap back, it might be weird for us to stay besties."

We stare at each other, and I hope she won't start crying or I'll start crying too. "Dana, what I'm trying to say is, I won't be offended if you get new friends who are your own age."

Dana looks down at the floor and gives a tiny nod. "Same here. I won't be offended if you get old people friends. You shouldn't have to cross-stitch alone. At least we're guaranteed this one last day together."

"I'm so glad we get to spend it with AZ8!" I scream, and we both jump around until my hips hurt.

A door slams in the distance and we shriek. The sound of footsteps in the hallway gets closer and closer until . . .

"Ms. Callus," I cry.

"Why are you both screeching like hyenas?" she asks curtly. "Did one of the ABCDEFG boys do something exhilarating, like peel a potato?"

"Are you being sarcastic?" I ask.

"Yes," she says, rolling her eyes.

"OK. So number one, AZ8 doesn't eat carbs on tour, because it slows their dancing down. And number two, why are you wearing your school uniform on a Saturday?"

"Because this uniform is stunning," she says as she does a little twirl. "Brown, tan, and mustard are such an underrated color combination, don't you think?"

"No," I say.

She's also wearing my dancing bunny ears hat again.

"And number three," Dana joins in, "what are you doing here?"

"I missed the place." She gazes fondly around the school hall like it's a long-lost friend. "Nana took pity on me and gave me a lift."

"Nana?"

"Yes, Nana. That woman would do anything for me. This is what happens when you're a devoted grandchild."

"Is this why you're here?" I ask. "To rub in my face how much my family loves you, even though they only love you because you're me?"

"I'm here because . . ." Ms. Callus begins, then stops as she looks down at her shiny black shoes. "Admittedly, I have enjoyed being young again, having a family, energy, and joints that don't creak with each movement. However, you're right. Your family loves you, not me. I've been selfish. I thought the swap could be a chance for me to start all over again, but I need to do that within my own life."

While hearing this makes me happier than seeing a photo of Woojin cuddling a puppy, it's also surprising. "Why the change of heart?"

"Last night, I had a girl-to-girl chat with Mommy."

"Mom only does the girl-to-girl chat thing when she's worried about me. Why was she worried?"

Ms. Callus takes out her phone and starts scrolling as if she hasn't heard me.

"Excuse me." I take it from her hand. "Tell me what Mom's worried about."

Ms. Callus folds her arms and tuts. "She told me that while she was proud of how I was taking a more active interest in studying and spending time with the family, she could see I had fundamentally *changed* without dance and the influence of the A80 Men."

"For the love of green energy," Dana shouts, "IT'S AZ8!"

Ms. Callus plays with a thread on her boxy brown blazer. "Mommy feels I've suddenly grown up too quickly, that I've lost some of my spark. She says passions are important and everyone must follow theirs."

While it's a very nice speech, I'm not sure I'm getting the gist of it. "So you're saying you want to be a Glow too?"

"No," she snaps. "What I'm saying is I have to find my own path, my own passions, my own friends, and to do that, I need to be myself again. I need to get my feet back into those beautiful Italian leather high heels and walk in them."

She wants to swap back! On hearing this I am filled with relief, and Dana and I start screaming and bouncing all over again.

Ms. Callus clears her throat impatiently. "I was led to believe time was of the essence."

"Yes," I say, "though how are we all going to get to Wembley Stadium by noon?"

Dana brings up a map on her phone. "We catch a bus, then another bus, then walk for nine minutes to the tube station and get the red line, then the purple line, then—"

"No, thank you," Ms. Callus says briskly. "I'm already traumatized from a week on local buses. I will not subject myself to further torture at the bacteria-covered hands of public transport. All that tinny music, crunching of chips and morning breath." She shudders. "I don't think I'll ever recover."

"I think what you're trying to say is you want me to book us a taxi." I wave the magical credit card in the air.

Ms. Callus snatches it away and tucks it into the pocket of her blazer. "No, what I'm trying to say is we're driving."

Dana and I follow Ms. Callus to her baby-pink vintage Jaguar and watch as she clicks a button and makes the roof roll back.

"Whoa," I exclaim as I chuck Ms. Callus's portrait in the passenger seat. "You're really going to let me drive this?"

She snorts. "Certainly not. I'm driving. You two, in the back and no snacking. I despise crumbs."

Even though it's a terrible shade of pink and the seats are covered in a jarring flowery pattern, I've never been in a convertible before and it feels so very bougie. Dana and I take a ton of *aegyo* selfies to document the occasion, especially when we hit the highway and the wind whips through Dana's long red mane and gently bounces off my own helmet hair. Then Woojin posts a selfie and we spend ages trying to work out what's going on under his hat.

"Dana, I think he has curtains again."

"No, that's a mullet—look closely."

"No way, it's a shadow; he's definitely gone short. Remember on the South American leg of the *Roses Are My Favorite Flower* tour, he—"

"Oh, do be quiet," Ms. Callus shouts from the front. "Do you have any idea how headache-inducing this babble is?" She puts on music from the olden days to "drown us out."

As cool as it is driving with the roof down, it's also very, very windy and I'm partially blinded by insects crash-landing in my eyes.

"What's our ETA?" Dana shouts.

"Don't worry, child. We will make it on time."

A police car pulls level beside us. Its officer takes a close look at the driver of our vehicle, and then a curious look at the giant oil painting of "me" in the passenger seat. The lights flash, and Ms. Callus slows down.

"What are you doing?" I yell.

"Finding a safe place to pull over so I can ascertain what this good man of the law wants."

"He probably wants to find out why a preteen is driving a vintage Jag on the highway."

"You could be right," Ms. Callus says. "I must not

risk getting into trouble. My record is impeccable."

"More importantly," I say, "we need to get to Wembley. The storm is literally going to pass over the stadium before making its way back out to sea."

Dana groans. "That defies meteorological sense."

"Sense?" Ms. Callus says. "Nothing about this situation makes sense." She slams the steering wheel as the siren rages beside us. "Darn it!" she shouts.

"Don't go slower," I urge. "Go faster."

Ms. Callus hits the gas so hard our heads fly back. Whoa, I did not see that coming. As we speed up, so does the police car.

Dana shrinks down and moans, "I'm starting to feel a little motion sickness here."

"Faster!" I yell. "Put that pedal to the metal, Ms. Callus; they're closing in on us."

We're now having an actual real-life car chase, and it's both super thrilling and terrifying. At one point the police car gets so close I can see the crumbs in the officer's beard. He glares at Ms. Callus in the front and his eyebrows knot in confusion. When he looks at me, I pull my best, most innocent smile, but I'm assuming my Ms. Callus smile isn't too charming because he scowls, lowers the window, and barks, "Pull over!"

Dana slides down farther in her seat. "I really

wish I didn't have lasagna for breakfast. I'm going to bring it back up any second . . ."

"You'll do no such thing," Ms. Callus shouts over the wind. "The upholstery in this vehicle is bespoke."

"Yikes," I squeal as a second police car appears and closes in on us. "Don't they have anything better to do on a Saturday morning?"

With both cars on our tail, I can see the panic on Ms. Callus's face. Though there's also a sparkle of something else, not quite confetti but perhaps . . . mischief?

"Ooh, I can feel it coming up," Dana moans. "Please, pull over."

"No, we can't," I cry. "Keep going. Keep going!"

Ms. Callus throws her head back and laughs; then she really goes for it, so fast I have to double-check that our seat belts are tightly fastened.

The sky darkens and the first drops of rain fall. This is it. This is the storm rolling in. But the clock is ticking; we've got to get to Wembley in the next fifteen minutes. We can't stop now.

We switch lanes sharply, leaving one of the police cars stuck behind a horse truck.

"Woo-hoo!" Ms. Callus screams. "My oh my, this is jolly great fun."

"Dana, do you want some water?"

"Yes please," Dana says, her face green. "Water might help dilute the vomit which is one hundred percent on its way up my esophagus."

"I feel so alive!" Ms. Callus shouts as she peels off the highway, losing the other police car.

We make a pit stop on a quiet road for Dana to quickly open the door and . . . well, she did indeed have lasagna for breakfast.

As we near Wembley Stadium, the crowds of Glows get bigger and denser. Everywhere there are AZ8 T-shirts, banners, light sticks, and, of course, dancing bunny ears hats. The sound of whistles being blown is both deafening and fabulous.

"Look at all these other Glows!" I could cry with happiness. "Finally we're with our people."

We pull to a stop and jump out of the car.

Ms. Callus points to a sign marked HOT FEET ARTISTS ENTRANCE and we leg our way over. I run as fast as I can to try to keep up with them—in my head I'm basically Usain Bolt—but my seventy-one-year-old body is having none of it.

"My identification!" I cry, racing back to grab the portrait from the passenger seat, and who would have thought gold frames could be so heavy? I lug it on my back, then spot two red-faced and puffing police officers pushing their way through crowds of confused Glows toward me.

"Oh no, no, please no," I cry as I try to muster some speed, but it's hard to run when you're carrying a giant oil painting of your own face.

"There she is!" they yell. "Stop that woman."

My heart pumps fast, my lungs burn, and my eyebrows sweat. Dana and Ms. Callus are way ahead, and I genuinely feel as if I'll never make it, as if my very last ounce of energy is almost used up, as if—

"Ooh, cool top," I puff as I pass a Glow wearing a limited-edition *The Moon Shines in Your Face* T-shirt.

She smiles back at me then does a double take. "No way! It's you. You're the K-popping principal. I'm a big fan. Huge."

"Thanks," I say between breaths, happy to meet a fan. "Can't really . . . stop because . . ."

Dana and Ms. Callus are nowhere to be seen, though behind me one of the officers definitely *can* be seen. Quite clearly and quite close.

"It's the K-popping principal," another Glow shouts.

Before I know it, there's a crowd of them asking me to sign stuff and do selfies while holding up my portrait. I oblige because I have manners and it's also exciting to be a celebrity.

"Police!" one of the officers yells.

"Sorry, guys," I say to my league of adoring fans, "but I'm in a rush. I need to get to the stage entrance side door."

The officer rudely pushes his way through hordes of Glows and is now super close. He holds his radio to his mouth and, I assume, calls for backup. Helicopters? Riot vans? What's the jail sentence for letting an eleven-year-old drive anyway?

"STOP THAT OLD WOMAN!" he screams.

I keep on running. No stopping. Please, feet, don't fail me now. The stage door is in sight. I'm going to make it. It's so close.

I lunge forward . . . just as a hand grabs me by the shoulder . . .

17
GREEN ROOM

"What do you think this is?" Ms. Callus pulls me through the door seconds before it slams shut, and I fall to the ground trying to catch my breath. "It was as if you were having a walk in the park. No sense of urgency at all."

I huff and puff. "I was trying. This painting is heavy, you know?"

A platinum-haired Korean lady asks me for my identification, and I have just about enough energy to hold the portrait up. She takes it from me with a strange look and waits till I catch my breath. "This way, please."

We're shown into something called a green room, which, surprise, surprise, isn't green at all but blue. It has lots of sofas and the longest snack table I've ever seen in my life.

I can't believe we're backstage at AZ8's concert.

It's exactly like my dreams, except in my dreams I'm not as stiff and wrinkly as this.

I grab a handful of Korean nibbles and eye up the competition. There are nineteen other "Hotter Feet" acts with us, including a ballerina, a pair of tap dancers, a street dance crew, and a guy in a very tight metallic suit whose specialty is doing really snappy movements with his feet while keeping the top half of his body absolutely still.

Garam was right when he said AZ8 was looking for variety, as the only thing any of this group has in common is how much of a big showy show they're making out of stretching.

"Don't you need to stretch too?" Ms. Callus asks me.

"Are you kidding? After that run, the only thing I need is a nice sit-down and some peace and qui—"

"Stop!" Dana orders as she puts her hands over my mouth. "Remember, being elderly is a state of mind."

I nod. "I don't need to stretch because I'm not a show-off like those guys."

"Yeah," Dana agrees. "What show-offs. Showing off with all their warm-up exercises."

"Stupid leg stretches."

"Yeah, so stupid. You can stretch way better than them. You could outstretch them with your eyes closed."

A woman enters and introduces herself as Kim Ji-Woo, AZ8's manager, to which we all ooooh because what could be better than managing eight global superstars?

"Thank you for coming," she says.

"There is literally nowhere else I'd rather be right now," Dana whispers in my ear. "Except maybe the UN Climate Change Conference."

"AZ8 is so excited to share a stage with you amateurs during their performance of 'Hot Feet.'"

Dana and I squeeze hands and go *"Eeeee!"* because this is getting very real and very exciting, very quickly.

Manager Kim continues, "Dance your hearts away, but please do not, under any circumstances, attempt to touch anyone from the band."

"Bummer," Dana mumbles.

"Lastly, because of the terrible weather in your country, the stage is quite slippery. Be careful, as we're liable for any injuries. Have fun and remember to sparkle like confetti." Manager Kim bows to signal the end of her speech.

We sit on the sofas and wait for the show to begin. It feels like time is slowing to a halt and the anticipation is so intense it makes me feel sick. Is the swap-back going to work? Will the lightning hit in the right place? Will Dig-D's hair stay in place if he does a front flip?

I busy myself trying to guess which of AZ8's back catalog of 136 songs they will perform first, while Dana explains to the man in the tight metallic suit how artificial fabric dyes are related to environmental degradation.

I notice Ms. Callus sitting alone. Why? There's a roomful of people here, yet she's not talking to anyone. I think of what Coach Cathy said to me in the staff room, how Ms. Callus never speaks to any of the other teachers. It doesn't make sense, because she's obviously liked being with people since she's been me. She's enjoyed hanging out with my family, dancing with my friends at the ninth-grade party and even joined the After-School Academics Club. So what stops her from being with people when she's the real her?

I go over and take a seat beside her. "Can I ask you a question?"

She sniffs. "If you must."

"Did you always want to be a principal?"

She huffs and fusses with the pumps on the dancing bunny ears hat. "What do you mean *want*?"

"Was it always your dream?"

She crosses her legs neatly at the ankles. "Leading Saint Margaret's was my ancestral duty. You could say I've been a principal since the day I was born."

"That's super weird, but OK." I take a sip of pear-flavored kombucha and think about what Mom said to Ms. Callus, that passions are important and everyone must follow theirs. I've always assumed being a mean, pushy, and terribly dressed principal was Ms. Callus's passion. But after the last few days, I'm no longer sure.

"So, hypothetically, if you didn't have to be a principal, what would you *like* to be?"

"Hypothetically?" Ms. Callus grins. "My, my, your vocabulary has improved this week. Well, let me think, if I was no longer a principal I would . . ." She chuckles. "There is one thing from the days of my youth I have always been interested in taking up again."

"And what's that? Bullying?"

"Modeling," Ms. Callus says.

"Modeling?" I repeat in surprise. "As in walking up and down a runway wearing an expensive dress and looking bored?"

"Why, yes. I know it's not a humble thing to say, but I've always been quite stunning." She takes my face in her hands. "Look at this: this bone structure, these eyes, this pure, raw charisma. It's perfection."

"Oh," I say, because, really, there are no other words.

"I did have a brief stint in my younger years as the official face of Chunky Monkey peanut butter."

Then it clicks; not just the sheer volume of cupboard space in her kitchen dedicated to peanut butter, but all the photos, paintings, and sculptures.

"You want to be a visual? Like Dig-C in AZ8. He sings and dances a little, but his main skill is being extremely pretty."

"And does this Diggy person get the summer off?"

Just as I'm about to tell Ms. Callus everything I know about AZ8's annual schedule, Dana comes over. "The storm is really getting going now. The Meteorological Office predicts it will peak at 2:20. I've also seen the set list for the show, and guess what song is due at that time?"

I clasp my hands together excitedly. "'Run, Run, Gotta Run Away from You, Baby'?"

"No," Dana says. "'Hot Feet.'"

I sigh. "Oh, yeah, of course."

"This is the plan: Skylar, you go onstage to dance, and when you see me wave like this"—Dana demonstrates her completely over-the-top wave—"Ms. Callus will run on, grab your hand, look deeply into your eyes and you'll both say all those heartfelt and meaningful things you said earlier about wanting to be yourselves again. Then—*snap, crackle, boom!*—you're back in each other's bodies. I mean, your own bodies. I mean, your original bodies. Yeah, something like that."

I feel a twinge in my stomach. Could it be nerves? Fear? Indigestion from eating three Korean hot dogs in twenty minutes? All this time I've been *excited* about going onstage with AZ8, dancing, and being hit by lightning, when really I should have been *terrified* about going onstage with AZ8, dancing, and being hit by lightning!

Dana puts her hands on my shoulders. "What's wrong, Skylar? Is the plan too confusing? Do you want me to storyboard it for you?"

"No. I'm just suddenly really scared about dancing out there. Because dancing is what got me into trouble in the first place."

"Actually, no," Ms. Callus says. "You defying school uniform policy by wearing this ridiculous but admittedly cute dancing bunny ears hat is what got you into trouble in the first place." She pulls it off and holds it out to me. "Here. I should never have taken it from you. It's just a hat. It's not as if it has any power over anything."

"Of course not," I agree.

"From now on, hats will be allowed as part of the Saint Margaret's school uniform," Ms. Callus announces.

"That's great news!" Dana says. "Though there's no way it's going to fit on your head right now, Skylar."

We both laugh as we try to wedge the hat over my giant helmet hair before giving up.

"Here, Dana, you can wear it."

"Thank you kindly," she says, making the ears dance before flinching. "Ouch! It gave me an electric shock. Did your nana buy this from Discounted Fake Stuff?"

I nod. "Yeah, it short-circuits sometimes."

"Good thing I won't be near any sources of strong electrical discharge this afternoon."

An announcement blares out over the speakers. "Show starts in ten minutes." I hear the crowd roar from inside the stadium. The next announcement is in Korean and causes everyone from the blue green room to shuffle out into the main backstage area. We follow too, but it's a bit squashed and disorienting with all the flashing lights and security people running around.

"What's going on?" Ms. Callus asks. "Why is there so much bated breath?"

"Shh," I whisper. "I think AZ8 is in the building. Though I don't know why we're all standing out here. It's not as if they're going to walk down this normal hallway, breathing all this normal air, like they're normal human beings. Right, Dana? Dana?"

Dana's mouth is open and she's deadly still.

Ms. Callus rolls her eyes. "Girls, how many more

times must I say this: they're just boys. Do you act this way around boys at our school?"

I pretend to puke. "No way. The boys at our school are disgusting. You can't put them in the same category as AZ8." I hold my hand in front of Dana's nose and mouth to make sure she's still breathing. Yep, we're all good. "Ms. Callus, haven't you learned anything this week? AZ8 aren't *just boys*; they're incredible musicians, dancers, songwriters, entertainers, rappers, representatives of their country, and—"

And there he is. Garam. In real life.

GARAM. HERE, IN ACTUAL REAL LIFE!

"No," I squeak.

Garam's face glows like the moon and there's a halo over his head. He's in full makeup and his hair falls stylishly over one eye.

"Dana, he's gone red," I gasp.

But when I look at Dana, she's already passed out and on the floor in a big heap. Again?! Why can't she keep it together? This is her chance to communicate with her bias.

Someone shouts, "Keep moving. Let the band through, please."

The other seven members of AZ8 step into view one by one. It's like the world switches to some kind of beautifully shot, slow-motion Oscar-winning movie and—

Whoa, is this real? Woojin turns, his diamond earrings sparkling in the light. He looks me straight in the eyes and says, "Rocking, popping principal."

His sweet, sweet voice is the last thing I hear.

18
SHOWTIME!

Something drips on my face. I'm not sure what. I'm not sure of anything really. There it is again, a drip of liquid. I wipe it off and hear Dana say, "I think she's waking up."

Waking up?

When was I asleep?

Though, my eyes *are* closed and I *am* lying down . . . but I'm not asleep because I can hear everything. I can hear Dana's voice, rain against windows, ninety thousand people screaming, and music. Oh, music. It's AZ8's "Illusions Are Not Real but They Are a Miracle." This is one of my favorite songs ever.

"Is this the live version?" I croak. "Someone turn it up."

Then another drip, this time right on my cheek. When I open my eyes, I see the super stretchy metallic-suited dancer leaning over me, his face running with sweat, which trickles off his forehead and right onto my—

"Yuck, gross!" I yell, sitting up. "Do you mind? You're perspiring on me."

"Sorry." He wipes an arm across his face. "I'm so hot from those stage lights."

"What stage lights?" I look around and realize *everyone* is sweating. They're panting and drinking water and have that typical exhausted and delighted look you get after dancing. Everyone except Dana and Ms. Callus, who sit on the floor next to me looking very glum.

"What?" I ask them. "What happened?" And with a wave of despair, it all comes back to me. "I passed out?"

They nod.

I grab Dana's arm and look at her watch. It's 2:37.

"I missed my chance to dance onstage with AZ8?"

Dana nods again. "Afraid so."

"I missed 2:22?"

"I'm sorry, Skylar."

I sink back down, devastated that because of my completely rational reaction to Woojin's natural beauty I'll now spend the rest of my life as a seventy-one-year-old and only ever see my family when the school holds parents' nights. "This is crushing." My voice wobbles.

"Yes," Ms. Callus says sadly. "It is so very disappointing."

I lie there and stare at the ceiling.

There's got to be another way. I can't be stuck like this forever, not when we've come so close. "Dana, is there a possibility the swap is a Monday-to-Sunday thing?"

"I wouldn't rule it out," she says.

My heart sinks. "I know that's your lying voice."

Her cheeks go red and she looks down at the floor.

This can't be it.

"I need to get back to being myself. I miss my body, my life, my bedroom, my family. I'm not going to give up," I say. "Missing one storm doesn't mean it's over. This is Britain; we have bad weather twelve months of the year."

"Exactly." Ms. Callus nods. Though she looks a little unsure.

I haul my elderly body up from the floor and give myself a shake.

"Is the old lady OK?" Manager Kim asks.

"She's fine," Ms. Callus says. "Just a little upset to have missed so much of the concert."

Manager Kim tips her head at me. "You remind me so much of my grandma. Come on, I know a good spot where you can watch the rest of the show."

We follow Manager Kim out through the backstage area and right to the side of the stage.

"Oh my Greta Thunberg!" Dana shrieks. "This is unbelievable."

AZ8 must be getting changed for the second half of the show, because the stage is empty with a black-and-white video montage playing on the big screens.

"I can't believe we're going to see AZ8's side profiles up close," Dana exclaims.

"Yeah, it's great," I say, trying to keep my voice bright. At the start of the week, I would've given anything to sit in the back row of this stadium; now I'm here, within spitting distance of AZ8, and I'm too distracted to enjoy it.

Manager Kim brings a folding chair and gestures for me to sit, but before I can say thank you, Ms. Callus swoops in and takes it with a sigh.

I get my phone out and check the weather forecast for the coming week. Nothing but sunshine. There's got to be another way.

The big screens fade to black, and the atmosphere fizzes. OK, maybe I *can* still enjoy this a little bit. The sea of raincoat-covered fans erupts into applause as a giant glittery golden star is slowly lowered onto the stage.

I shiver with goose bumps as I realize I recognize that star. It's the same one from the music video for

"Green Tea under the Trees." I can hardly breathe. Is Woojin going to do a solo?

"This is incredible!" I shout. "This is so special. This almost makes up for the whole my-life-being-ruined thing."

I feel my hand being squeezed, a little too tight. "Ouch!" I yelp, turning to Dana, who is flaming with anger. "Why are you trying to crush my bones? Let go!"

She growls and I follow her gaze across to the other side of the stage where Woojin has appeared, still hidden from the crowd. Whoa. He's wearing a white suit covered in rhinestones and a pair of bright green high-heeled boots. He looks completely surreal.

"Oh my," I murmur. The faint feeling returns, but there's no way I'm going to pass out with Dana gripping me so tightly.

"Woojin was just drinking from a single-use plastic bottle," she says through gritted teeth. "And now he's . . . he's . . ."

"Not really a human at all, but a literal angel? An alien from planet Perfect? An ethereal—"

"No!" she cries. "Now he's using a plastic spork."

She's right. Woojin is indeed eating some kind of meal with a disposable white plastic spork. Oh dear. He hands the food to an assistant, then grabs his microphone and runs onto the stage to deafening screams.

"The only way to get out of the climate crisis is to educate ourselves to do better," Dana says firmly.

"OK, well, *later* we can message Woojin on AZ8's socials."

Dana has this weird look in her eyes, like the time she superglued herself to our local library because they'd started leaving the lights on overnight.

"Dana, whatever you're thinking of doing . . . stop."

"Why wait till later? I need to tell him now."

"Right now? Are you sure it's not something that could wait?"

She shakes her head furiously. "The clock is ticking for planet Earth!" And with that she too runs onstage.

"Dana, no!" I yell.

"There is no planet B!" she screams at Woojin as he steps onto his glittery star and begins to sing.

"What is she doing?" Ms. Callus shouts. And she isn't the only one shouting, because all around me, people are freaking out and the whole thing is complete commotion.

"What's that kid in the counterfeit dancing bunny ears hat doing?"

"It's one of your students—do something!"

"Security!"

Woojin hasn't noticed Dana yet, and now the star is lifting from the stage.

"Yikes. No," I mutter. But also, a little bit yes! Because Woojin perched on a giant star and singing live is a thing of perfect loveliness. However, Dana grabbing on to the star and lifting up into the air with it . . . well, that's quite another matter.

Dana dangles over the stage and for a few seconds I can't breathe. Is this really a real thing that's happening in my real life?

Behind me, Manager Kim says, "The star is programmed to fly almost a hundred feet in the air. We need to get an ambulance on standby."

An ambulance? Visions of Dana falling from the star shock me into action and, without thinking, I too sprint onstage. There's no way I'm letting my bestie get hurt.

My feet nearly go out from under me, and I scramble to keep my balance. "Wow, it's slippery up here," I mumble.

I stand under the star and look up as it lifts higher and higher. Dana's shoes are the only thing within reaching distance, so as Woojin belts out the infamous line *"Stars are beautiful and every country has them,"* I jump and manage to grab on to one foot.

I honestly don't know if the crowd's going wild because Woojin sounds so super adorable or because there are two complete randoms hanging from the star.

Did I say two? Because actually I mean three . . .

"Ouch!" I cry as Ms. Callus grabs hold of my waist and the three of us soar above the stage. "What are you doing?" I scream down.

"I'm in loco parentis," she screams back up.

"I don't know what that means!"

"It's the teachers' code. It means while your parents aren't here, I'm them."

"That's so dumb," I yell. "My parents would never let me do this."

Suddenly a huge flash lights up the sky, followed by a massive clap of thunder. Oh, the storm *is* still going!

Above me, Dana shouts, "Woojin, do you know plastic bottles are responsible for seven percent of plastic waste in the world's oceans?"

The rain falls fast.

"Little Miss Skylar," Ms. Callus hollers, "please try not to land on my beautiful face if you fall."

The crowd roars, light sticks flash, and Woojin sings, *"Stars are so pretty and shiny like meeee."*

If I wasn't hanging a bajillion feet over a stage, I would totally get a tingly spine from hearing it.

"Stars in your eyes are my cup of green teaaaa—"

Woojin kneels down toward Dana and takes one of the dancing bunny ears pumps in his hand.

I am never going to wash that hat again.

"Woojin!" Dana shouts. "I wish I could show you there's a more sustainable way to live. I wish you would come to my school and see the eco-changes we've made."

Woojin, still playing with the hat, croons ever so beautifully, *"Get the stars and the tea and we'll both climb the treeee."*

There's a flash of lightning, so sharp and so stunning that I squeeze my eyes shut. When I manage to reopen them, I'm almost blinded by Woojin's star as it crackles with green light. Boy, AZ8 really blew the budget on the pyrotechnics for this show. Even Woojin himself is sparkling with green light.

Actually . . . so is Dana. She looks down at me and cries, "I feel weird!"

The ears on the dancing bunny hat are flapping wildly. "No matter what happens, you're still my bestie," she screams down.

"You're still my bestie too," I scream up.

"I wish you weren't an old lady anymore!" she shouts.

The green light turns white as it swallows us up: me, Dana, Ms. Callus and Woojin. The star twirls and whirls, it spins and turns, and then . . . *BOOM!*

We fall to the stage in a shower of tiny silvery stars.

✦ ✦ ✦

"What happened?" I croak, but my voice is lost to a weird fizzing sound and then the crowd chanting, "We want more! We want more!"

I crawl over to find Dana. "Are you OK?"

"I'm OK. Are you OK?" She grabs me by the arms and stares very closely at my face. "Is it really you, Skylar?"

"I don't know." I touch my face—smooth and supple; my hair—curly and soft; and my body—young and eleven.

ELEVEN!

YES!

"I'm back!" I cry. "I'm back! I'm back!"

From the side of the stage Manager Kim screams into a walkie-talkie, "Security! The old-lady principal has gone *michyeosseo*!"

I turn to look for Ms. Callus, but before I spot her Dig-D and Dig-C run onstage wearing business suits and jewel-encrusted open-toed sandals, and I scream with excitement. The opening bars of "Time Stands Still When We Hold Hands" play and they break into a synchronized dance routine. This is epic!

Garam, the only member of AZ8 who speaks fluent English, skips over, looking simply perfect in a pair of red velvet overalls. "Why is your principal trying to fight Woojin?" he asks, pointing over at a scuffle.

I rub my eyes because he's right: Ms. Callus *is* trying to fight Woojin. Yes, that's what I said. My principal, who is thankfully back in her own old-lady body, is pushing and slapping AZ8's lead singer and five-time ABCDGVP Award-winning superstar Woojin.

"Security!" someone shouts.

"It's that helmet-haired principal from the internet," another calls. "Stop her!"

Ms. Callus tackles Woojin to the ground as she tries to get his microphone. Why is this happening? I need to get involved and stop it. I need to help. I need to—

"Dance?"

I look up and there he is: Dig-D. He offers his hand and repeats, "Dance?"

"Yes," I say, completely ecstatic, because who wouldn't be?

Dig-D helps both me and Dana to our feet and we mimic his moves. Onstage. In front of everyone.

"This is amazing!" I shout.

Dana grins. "I know!"

We copy Dig-D's running man then stand back as he demonstrates the greatest front flip I've ever witnessed; and yes, his hair does stay in place.

"You did it, Dana," I call over the music. "But how?"

"I don't know," she says. "I just wished for you to be back and it worked."

"You're a genius," I sing as I throw my arms around her.

"That's a very common misconception about me."

Right then, Jungwon moonwalks over to us and takes the dancing bunny ears hat from Dana. He puts it on his own head and indicates for us to take a selfie with him. Yes, a selfie with actual, literal, whole Jungwon.

"I think he's my new bias," Dana says as he dances off to the front of the stage.

"Me too," I agree as I do the backward shuffle.

I spot Ms. Callus being dragged away by a gang of huge burly security guards, and, as much as this is the single greatest moment of my life, it's also the single weirdest.

"We need to help Ms. Callus," I say.

Dana nods and we run offstage, following the security guards to the exit, where they open the door and shout, "Get out and stay out, you weird fan!" before tossing Ms. Callus onto a pile of trash bags.

"Wait," I call. "We're leaving too."

Dana and I run outside, then turn to watch as the door to AZ8 is slammed shut.

From inside we hear the sounds of "Beauty Is the Beast I Love" and Dana fake-cries. "This is my most favorite AZ8 song ever."

"I know," I say. "I'm sorry you're missing it."

She smiles at me. "Doesn't matter. Nothing will ever top dancing onstage with them. Except of course a climate-neutral future for all." She nods down to Ms. Callus, who is rolling around in a burst trash bag of half-eaten hot dogs and crushed drinks cups. "Do you think she's all right?"

"Must be tough getting used to her old-lady body again."

We pull Ms. Callus from the stinking trash and sit her up.

"Are you OK?" I ask.

She looks up at us both, then makes this movement like she's trying to push a loose bit of hair from her face, which is weird because I don't believe the helmet hair has ever been soft enough to come loose. There's also something familiar about the way she does it.

"MS. CALLUS?" I shout as we kneel down in front of her. "Are you OK?"

"Maybe the lightning strike put her into shock," Dana muses. "Or perhaps those security guards hurt her. If so, we can sue them."

Ms. Callus looks over our shoulders at the stage door, then back at us and says, *"Annyeonghaseyo."*

"Uh, what now?" I ask.

"Annyeonghaseyo," she repeats.

"Dana, do you happen to recognize what language Ms. Callus is speaking right now?"

"Hmm, well, I'm no expert in foreign languages . . ."

"Yes, you are, and we all know you are."

We stare back at Ms. Callus.

Could it be?

No. No way.

"Dana," I say slowly, "when you were hanging off that star, you wished for me to be me again, right?"

"Yes."

"What else did you wish for?"

She bites her lip and her eyes widen. "I wished that Woojin could come and see our school."

"Showtime?" Ms. Callus, who I'm no longer sure is really Ms. Callus, says. Then, again, the weird pushing back of hair where there is NO HAIR.

I don't even want to say it out loud, because saying it out loud is almost as good as admitting it. But the fact is, Ms. Callus *is* speaking Korean right now.

Dana's cheeks are red. "Don't say it, Skylar."

"I won't . . . but—"

"Don't," she warns me.

Ms. Callus flicks her head.

"It's almost like . . ." I begin. "Well, it's almost like she believes she has a full head of luscious thick hair cut in a style that needs to be temptingly flicked away."

We jump up.

Dana croaks, "Please tell me I'm wrong about the thing I know you know I'm thinking of."

We take some deep breaths, then kneel back down in front of Ms. Callus. I take her old hand—which thanks to my rigorous moisturizing regime is now softer than a baby's bottom—and ask, "Can you tell me what your name is?"

Ms. Callus pouts and answers, "Park Woojin. You want autograph?"

19
ONE MONTH LATER

Dana sits on the sofa with me and Kookie, who weirdly has decided she no longer eats fish and will only tolerate beef or chicken. And let me tell you, that combination on the breath is an absolute treat.

Dad jogs into the room in his bright red running shoes, still pristine, and tries to touch his toes.

"Right then, girlies, who's coming for a run with me?"

"No way," I say, opening a bag of chips. "AZ8 is about to premiere the video for 'Ring, Ring, Pick Up the Phone, It's Me.'"

"Didn't that already happen? I'm sure last week I was subjected to that song for many, many hours. *It's me on the phone, baby, la la la*," he sings tunelessly.

"Please," I groan. "Stop this madness."

Dana laughs. "Told you we should have watched it at my house."

"We can watch it in my bedroom if you want?" I offer.

Dana shakes her head. "No. Your bedroom is the tiniest room ever made and it gives me claustrophobia."

"Anyway, Dad, what we watched last week was the official snowsuit music video. Tonight is the beach version of the Japanese version of the official remix."

Dana squeals. "I hope they show Tae swimming."

"Me too. He looks so cute when he swims, like a baby seal."

I'm no longer Woojin biased. No one is. Ever since he and Ms. Callus swapped bodies, he's become more of a backing member of the band . . . although he still gets the most screen time in their videos for being a fashionista. In their last video for "Teach Me How to Be Your Top Student" he was rocking a crazy new hairstyle called "the helmet" and a flowery cardigan that sold out across the world in seconds. As does Chunky Monkey peanut butter every time he's spotted eating it from the jar.

And as for the *real* Woojin, well, he seems to love his new life as principal of Saint Margaret's Academy, especially the anonymity of it. His favorite thing to do is walk down the street without being followed by crowds of screaming fans or go to the supermarket and steal the odd grape without it being filmed and going viral.

Dad groans as Dana turns up the volume. "Don't worry, Leafy," he whispers to his little bonsai, which still hasn't grown, "once they're gone, I'll get the vinyl out and play you some real music."

"What are we watching, girls?" Mom asks as she wanders in. "Oh no!" She grabs the chips off me. "More K-pop. When will this stage end?" She plops herself on the sofa and rolls her eyes. Though, as much as she pretends to hate AZ8, I caught her humming their smash hit single "Let Me Sew You a Heart" when we went swimming together last Wednesday.

Dad drops the pretense of going for a run and sits down next to Mom, and, just as it's getting really squashed on the sofa, Nana joins too. At least she brings food.

"Kimchi-and-cheese burrito?" she says, handing one to each of us.

"Ooh," Dana coos. "These are amazing. You should have a food truck."

"Skylar made the kimchi," Nana says, nudging my shoulder and smiling.

I used to hate having to help Nana in the kitchen, but a week of takeouts helped me appreciate home-cooked food. Plus, it's kind of nice hanging out with Nana sometimes.

She brings up a page on her phone from Discounted Fake Stuff with the new range of dancing bunny ears hats in neon. I never saw my hat again after Jungwon danced away with it at Wembley Stadium. I don't mind him having it; I just hope he never wears it during a thunderstorm while wishing for something he hasn't thought through . . .

"You want a new one?" Nana asks me.

I look at Dana and we both laugh.

"No thanks," I reply, "and here's a thousand reasons why—"

"Shh," Dad says. "The video is about to start."

Skylar's K-pop Dictionary

AEGYO
The act of extreme cuteness.

AZ8
The most amazing boy band of all time.

BIAS
Your favorite member.
(Mine is obviously Woojin!)

BIAS WRECKER
The member who unexpectedly catches your attention.

COMEBACK
The launch of a new music video, song, or album.
(Get ready for amazingness!)

GLOW
The greatest fandom of the greatest band.
I LOVE AZ8!

MAKNAE
The youngest of a band, or in Saint Margaret's case, the sixth graders.

MERCH
Don't buy it on the Discounted Fake Stuff site!

STAN

Be appropriately obsessed with something.

(e.g. I stan Woojin because he is amazing.)

VISUAL
The most beautiful band member.

HARU

Special move: Triple backflip

Holds the record for: Longest rap solo while breakdancing

SKYLAR ♡ WOOJIN

TAE

Signature look: Dimples that have their own GPS coordinates

Eco-mission: To save the planet from avocados

DIG-D

Signature look: Open-toed sandals

Holds record for: Performing a front flip without a single hair out of place

YUJUN

Special move: High notes

Fun fact: His large vocal range allows him to sing with dolphins.

WOOJIN

Special move: Hair flick

Fun fact: Was Under-12 UNO champion

GARAM

Signature look: A perfectly placed beauty mark that has its own live stream

Fun fact: Can sing "We Don't Talk About Bruno" in seventeen languages

JUNGWON

Signature look: Flawless fringe

Holds the record for: Most views ever on AZ8's live channel—22.2 million people watched "How I get my hair to look this good."

DIG-C

Special move: Looking pretty

Fun fact: Made a whole stadium cry at his aegyo smile

ACKNOWLEDGMENTS

Thank you to my agent, Eve White, for having that **BOOMBAYAH** for Skylar and her K-pop adventures from the very first phone call. And to Ludo Cinelli for having the **DDU-DU DDU-DU** enthusiasm.

Whoa, Megan Middleton, you truly are the most **DYNAMITE** editor and I have loved the **FIRE** you've brought to the **DNA** of each edit.

Huge shout-out to Denise Johnstone-Burt and the whole Walker Books team for being **THUNDEROUS**. I truly have a **CASE 143** working with you all. Also, to my eagle-eyed copyeditor, Georgie Hookings, thank you so **MUMUMUMUCH**.

All the applause to Amy Nguyen for the **VERY NICE** and **SUPER** illustrations—you really brought Skylar and Ms. Callus to life. And to **HYPE BOY** Jamie Hammond for all the work on the book design—it's just so **OMG**.

Finally, a million finger hearts to all the fangirls and fanboys out there. While it's the music that dragged me down the K-pop rabbit hole, it's you who give me **THE FEELS**. I **LIKEY** you all very much, even when you're encouraging me to spend too much time online, dance till three a.m., or fly to the other side of the world to take photos outside of a seemingly random office building in Seoul.

About the Author

LUAN GOLDIE is a writer of children's books as well as short stories and novels for adults. She worked in elementary schools for over a decade, where she loved teaching PE and anything that involved clay, paint, or glitter.

When not writing, Luan can be found teaching writing to others, hanging upside down at a fitness class, or watching K-pop music videos. Her ult bias is Kim Namjoon from BTS.